# SEASONS IN OUR TIME

Hillary Griffin

Copyright © 2023 Hillary Griffin

All rights reserved

The characters and events portrayed in this book are fictitious. Any similarity to real persons, living or dead, is coincidental and not intended by the author.

No part of this book may be reproduced, or stored in a retrieval system, or transmitted in any form or by any means, electronic, mechanical, photocopying, recording, or otherwise, without express written permission of the publisher.

ISBN-13: 9798373954112

Cover design by: Hillary Griffin

# CONTENTS

Title Page
Copyright
Foreword — 1
Unexpected beginnings — 2
Lockdown — 10
A Different Kind of War — 11
Home School — 18
Day Trip — 26
The Last Sister — 36
September morning — 43
Race against Time — 45
The Red Coat — 58
The Drive In — 66
Take Three Dads — 76
Spring Blooms — 81
Appendix — 90

# FOREWORD

At the beginning of 2020, very few people suspected that daily life in many parts of the world was about to change dramatically, due to a virus that had emerged in China. By April, however, most Europeans had accepted lockdowns of varying degrees of severity as the COVID 19 pandemic swept across the continent. As I write this, in late 2022, daily life has returned to "pre COVID" conditions.

Prior to 2020, the last pandemic to have a major impact on Europe was the Spanish 'flu of 1918 to 1919 and it was largely overshadowed by the end of World War I. As we start to forget the details of how our lives were changed in 2020, I decided that I wanted to find some way of recording those days. This is not a historical record, but rather, stories of ordinary people living through 2020, adapting their lives to the restrictions that were in force at any given point during the year. The pandemic affected so many aspects of ordinary life, from shopping to transport, employment to leisure activities. In contrast to 1918, the restrictions imposed on populations were more far reaching but modern technology enabled people to stay connected, meeting online for social interaction as well as work, school, worship and recreation.

A number of words entered our vocabulary which no doubt will soon cease to have the meaning that they did for that short period of time: "lockdown", "social distancing", "furlough", "tier system", "track and trace". I have provided a brief summary of the COVID related events in the UK from February 2020, the date of the first story in the collection, through to April 2021 in the Appendix.

# UNEXPECTED BEGINNINGS

*February 2020, West Lancashire*

"OK, ladies, super stuff, just one last time from the top," our choir leader encouraged. The chorus of "Make Your Own Kind of Music" reverberated around the community hall.

Chairs were scraped back, amidst a babble of conversations as the rehearsal ended.

"Have you sorted out your travel insurance now?"

"Can you manage to get everything in your hand luggage?"

"I bet your parents will spoil the children rotten while you're away."

I hurried out of the hall, conscious of how much I had to do at home and at work before our flight to Milan on Friday evening. The cold February night air made me gasp for breath, but I was glad that I had walked the short distance to the hall, and didn't have to stand in the cold scraping ice off a car windscreen. The last thing I wanted at this stage was to go down with a cold, or even worse, 'flu.

On Friday evening, our group's minibus arrived at Manchester Airport well ahead of schedule. We were able to enjoy a pre-flight glass of wine to celebrate the start of our week-end adventure. Louise had never taken a choir abroad and we were looking forward to sightseeing and window shopping in Milan, as well as performing our set list at two venues. Three hours later we landed in Italy, impressed by the slick organisation at the sprawling Malpensa Airport.

The week-end passed all too quickly, with an abundance of good food and wine, a trip to the renowned cathedral, an afternoon window shopping for clothes and shoes which we could only dream of wearing, and of course, taking part in two concerts. All too soon we were sitting in the Departure Lounge at Malpensa Airport on Sunday evening.

"Are you back in the office tomorrow, Jo?" asked Louise.

"Yes, afraid so, it's hard to get annual leave at this time of year, with so many companies needing to file accounts by the end of March," I replied.

"I've got a shift too," said my friend Alice. "It's just lucky the school's taken an inset day at the end of half-term, so at least the children can have an extra day with my parents and I won't have the school run to do."

"I'm surprised we haven't seen more school parties…a lot of the private schools run skiing trips in February and they must use this airport."

"Hm … my boys were due to go, but the trip was cancelled," commented Georgina. Her husband was a corporate lawyer so they could well afford the fees for the local private school. "The headteacher was very cautious about this COVID thing."

"What, this Chinese virus? That's thousands of miles away."

Before anyone else could chip in, Louise interrupted, "Look, we've been called to the gate, we'd better get going. Has everyone got their passports and boarding cards handy?" Louise reverted to organiser mode as she corralled our group in the direction of our gate.

And so ended our trip, with another hassle-free flight, arriving in Manchester ten minutes ahead of schedule.

It was hard to wind down after the busy week-end and I was awake long before the radio-alarm burst into life at 6.15am. A quick shower, a slice of toast and I was out of the house in time to catch the 7.30am commuter train, arriving in the office by 8.15am. The city streets were still quiet at this time, with just a few rough sleepers huddled under sleeping bags in doorways.

The office was stiflingly warm as I came in from the cold morning air, and I tried to dismiss the dry ticklish feeling at the back of my throat with the first coffee of the morning. Just settle down to that urgent set of accounts, I told myself, and you'll forget about that.

"Are you sure you're OK, Jo?" my colleague Sue asked at lunch time. "You're coughing an awful lot, maybe you picked something up on the flight. I always come home with a cold after a trip abroad."

"I'm fine, it's just the dry air in here."

"You should have taken today off, given yourself time to recover after the week-end."

"I didn't want to start dipping into my annual leave so early in the year; and besides, we'll struggle to get everything done that we need to before the end of March as it is."

"Well, as long as you don't pass any of those Italian germs onto me…"

The afternoon seemed to drag on and I was increasingly conscious of trying to suppress the urge to cough. I resorted to paracetamol and fruit tea, wishing that I had some honey to soothe my throat. Eventually the digital display on my desk top computer tripped over to 17.00 and I felt no compunction in switching off and making a bee line for the door.

"Ah, Jo, could I just have a word…"

I turned to see one of the partners emerging from his office.

"Well…"

"I've just taken a call from the new Finance Director at Hall's, we need to arrange a meeting to discuss some queries on last month's management accounts."

"My diary is fully up to date," I bit my lip, not wanting to sound too abrupt. "Is it something Carina could sort out in the morning?"

"I'd rather get back to him straight away, make a good impression. We wouldn't want him to start talking to the firm his previous company used. I was thinking of Wednesday morning, we'd go to his office of course."

My heart sank. Hall's premises were on the other side of the city, so by the time we got back to the office, half a day would have been wasted on a few queries that could have been dealt with by email. Still, we couldn't afford to upset a good client.

"OK, I haven't got any appointments on Wednesday morning."

"Excellent, I'll say we'll be there at 9.30. We'll need to spend a few minutes going through the key figures in the management accounts tomorrow afternoon too so that I'm fully up to speed. And have we got a handle on their current tax position?"

"I'll speak to Andrea in the morning."

"Great, don't let me hold you up any longer."

Martin turned back into his office and I dashed out through reception before anyone else could waylay me. As I rushed to the station, I was aware of the cold air making me cough more often.

The following morning, I was rudely awakened by the radio alarm. I felt incredibly hot although the heating had not even switched on yet. I staggered to the bathroom and dosed myself up with paracetamol. I was still coughing yet had no sign of a head cold.

I decided that this was an opportune time to make use of the facility to log on to the office systems and take part of the morning to "Work from Home", hoping that the paracetamol would work their magic and I would be able to get into the office for this afternoon's meeting.

Amazingly, I was feeling much better by lunch time; the coughing fits were less intense and I returned to the office in much better spirits than I had left the previous afternoon. The meeting with Martin took up far less time than I had expected and by the end of the day I had completed the final set of accounts that were due to be filed by the end of February. With a sigh of relief, I left behind a desk that was a model for the "clean desk" policy.

"Well Jo, that was the best coffee I've had for a long time, and it was a real treat to sample some of their new biscuit lines," remarked Martin as we left Hall's premises the following morning.

"I'm afraid my sense of taste isn't too good at the moment, but the biscuits certainly looked very upmarket."

"It's a pity you hadn't got the tax numbers from Andrea though, it's not like you to forget."

Drat, I had meant to speak to Andrea the previous morning but totally forgotten about it when I was working at home. "I'm sorry Martin, I'll catch up with her as soon as we get back in and email an update over to the FD."

My phone beeped, demanding my attention. I quickly read the text from my friend, Alice. "Choir rehearsal cancelled. Give me a call when you're free."

That was odd; we had a lot of material to rehearse before our spring concert. I listened absently while Martin continued to enthuse about Hall's new biscuit range and called Alice as soon as we were back in the office.

"Hi, Alice, are you OK?"

"I'm fine Jo. I just wanted to get a message to you in case you were working late and didn't get chance to check your personal email. Tonight's choir practice has been cancelled. Louise has gone down with some bug."

"I must admit, I was feeling pretty awful on Monday. I even worked from home yesterday morning as my temperature seemed a bit high, but I feel much better now. "

"Apparently loads of people have got a really bad cough, so they don't feel up to singing, and being asthmatic, Louise always seems to be worse with these winter viruses."

"I guess we must have picked something up on the plane; it's not unusual when everyone's breathing in the same air in an enclosed space for three hours, it's worse than the train."

"Well, I'm just glad I haven't got any symptoms; can you imagine if I'd come home with a virus and passed it onto the kids, let alone Gareth and my parents? There'd be no more trips away with the choir for me."

"There are some advantages to being on your own. Anyway, thanks for letting me know. It'll give me chance to stay on a bit in the office this evening as I've been out at a meeting all morning."

"Honestly Jo, take it easy. Meeting your clients is work too you know."

"Yes, but there's just so much to get through before the end of March. I'll catch up with you at the week-end."

"OK, perhaps we could go for a coffee after Parkrun?"

"Good idea. Let's do that."

The next three weeks passed by in a blur. The spring concert was rapidly approaching and I had tried to remember to listen to the songs on my phone during the commute to and from the office. By mid- March, Louise seemed relatively pleased with our progress. I was still working long hours and paying scant attention to the news about the likelihood of a lockdown and the growing number of cases of COVID.

I was about to leave the office one Monday evening when Martin came to look for me.

"I've just been talking to the FD from Hall's. He was in quite a state, his mother has suddenly passed away."

"I'm sorry to hear that, had she been ill?"

"Not really, she was very active, looked after his children after school and all that. Sounds as if she had something like pneumonia and it was all very quick. Anyway, I'll get Carina to send some flowers. "

"I don't think she's been in today. She phoned in sick this morning."

"Hmm…she was in London last week-end. I hope she hasn't picked up this COVID virus. I think we'll all be working from home more before too much longer."

"I suppose so. It'll be difficult for clients…."

"That might be the least of our worries if it's as bad here as in northern Italy."

He disappeared back into his office.

Later that evening, I watched Boris Johnson's statement on TV. It was a grim message: no non-essential social contact, work from home if possible, no unnecessary travel and 12 weeks' isolation for the over 70s and medically vulnerable.

My phone beeped.

"Jo, it's Alice. Have you seen the TV?"

"Yes, it's a bit of a shock. Martin was only saying earlier that we'd soon be working from home more."

"I don't know how we're going to cope. How can Gareth run a restaurant when people have been told not to socialise?"

"I guess this is only the start of announcements. I'm still trying to get my head around it all: no choir, no Parkrun…"

"Poor Louise, she'll have to suspend our subscriptions but then she'll have no money coming in. "

"At least it's March, it's not as if it's December. These viruses are always worse in the winter and we should be back to normal by June."

"Umm, I've been thinking. You know that cough that so many people had after we went to Milan, you don't think that was COVID do you?"

"Well, no one was very ill, were they? Surely COVID symptoms are worse than that or they wouldn't be going to these lengths to keep people apart?"

"Honestly Jo, haven't you been listening to anything? It's pretty mild for most people but it's just so infectious that if millions of people catch the virus the number who are seriously ill will be... well, a big number. You're the numbers person, work it out."

"Fair point."

"Look, I'd better go. The kids are fighting again. You're not going into the office tomorrow, are you?"

"I don't know, I'd better keep an eye on my email. I really can't see how I could manage to do everything I need to from home for the next three months."

"Well, take care, remember your health's more important than those deadlines of yours."

"You too. I was going to say see you soon, but I guess I won't. Keep in touch."

"Yes, of course. Bye."

# LOCKDOWN

*March 2020*

Saturday morning, streets deserted
No sport today, all is cancelled
Supermarket shelves stripped bare
Hurried shoppers, no time to spare

Sunday dawns, no church bells ringing
Postponed, Mothering Sunday gatherings
The sun shines on in clear blue skies
Another COVID patient dies

Monday, the PM pronounces
Stay at home, do not take chances
"Hands, face, space" the latest watchwords
Weeks of lockdown stretch before us

Spring advances, our gardens thrive
Keep close to home and do not drive
No more overseas vacations
We must stay in isolation

## A DIFFERENT KIND OF WAR

*March 2020, Majorca*

There was a bump as the aeroplane touched down on the Palma runway. The elderly gentleman in the next seat started rummaging through a khaki shoulder bag with multiple zippered pockets.

"Ah, got them," he said triumphantly as he pulled out two claret passports. "Only another year and we'll get proper passports again, I mean blue British passports like we used to have. I expect you're too young to remember them," he added, turning to me.

"No, not at all," I answered, pulling my own passport out of my handbag, as passengers in the rows ahead of us started to get up and reach up to the overhead lockers for their hand luggage.

"That one looks a bit different," the man commented, glancing at my passport.

"Yes, it's Spanish."

"Really? Your English is very fluent."

"I've lived in England most of my adult life, but my father was Spanish."

"Oh, I see. Well, at least you won't have to worry about going over the 90 day limit for visits. Every cloud has a silver lining."

"Yes…I think we're moving now. I hope you enjoy your holiday."

I moved into the central aisle and looked determinedly in front of me, not wanting to prolong the conversation with my neighbour. I wondered if he would be quite so keen on his British passport once he realised that he would be queuing at Immigration Control for an entry stamp on future visits, after Brexit was fully implemented.

I hurried on, anxious to catch the Airport Bus to the City Centre and board a bus to Alcudia before the lunch-time hiatus. I hardly spared a glance at the new signs urging passengers to wash their hands frequently and to cover their faces when coughing or sneezing.

It was a mild day for early March and the journey passed without incident. The weak spring sunshine lit up the blossom covered trees and honey coloured stone walls. In the distance I could clearly see the peaks of the Tramuntana mountains as the bus sped across the island. By mid- afternoon we had reached the outskirts of Alcudia; my heart beat faster as I strained for a first glimpse of my apartment block, handily situated on the road to the coast.

Home…or to be more precise, second home…at last. I heaved my small suitcase up the stairs to the first floor and unlocked the door of my flat. I opened the windows, unlatched the shutters and looked out towards the slopes of the headland rising towards the lofty Talaia d'Alcudia. I would need to look at the local weather forecasts and work out a plan for my hikes over the next few weeks before the influx of tourists at Easter. But first, time to check out which cafes were open and enjoy a decent cup of coffee and slice of almond cake before restocking with groceries.

Later that evening, I phoned my mother, now in her late 80s and settled in a well- run residential home on the outskirts of Madrid. She had not wanted to return to her native Devon after my father's death, having lived in Spain for over fifty years.

"Ana, where are you?"

"I'm in my flat in Alcudia, you remember I told you I would be coming over in March."

"And when are you coming to Madrid?"

I sighed; it was unlike my mother to be so abrupt and anxious. "I'll come before Easter, at the beginning of April; that way I can avoid the crowds here."

"I think you'll be too late."

"Whatever do you mean, are you alright?"

"Yes, I'm fine but I am worried you may not be able to visit. More and more people have this new virus."

"I don't think it's anything to worry about. It's milder than the 'flu from what I've heard, and you've never had any problems with your chest."

"Hm…I am 86 you know."

"Well, I'll keep an eye on the news. There are flights to Madrid every day."

We chatted on for a few minutes longer and then I said good night to my mother; the early flight from Manchester was taking its toll and I suddenly felt extremely tired. In the rush to prepare for my three months away from the UK, I had paid scant attention to newspaper reports about the threat posed by the COVID virus which had resulted in an unprecedented lockdown in the Chinese city of Wuhan and was now spreading westwards across Europe.

The following morning, I awoke to a beautiful early spring day. I breakfasted quickly, packed a ham and cheese baguette into my walking rucksack and set out along the coast. The holiday villas and hotels were still firmly shuttered and I only passed the occasional dog walker and a few retired couples. By mid-day I had reached the highest point of my walk and looked out over the Bay of Alcudia, stretching into the distance.

As I returned along the road to my flat, I saw my neighbour, Stanley, a retired expat who spent most of the year on the island.

"Ana, good to see you again. How long are you here for?"

"Three months; I'm hoping for a good few days' walking before I go to Madrid to see my mother."

"Haven't you seen the national news? This COVID virus is spreading rapidly in Madrid, I think they'll be introducing quarantine zones like the ones in northern Italy soon."

"No, I only arrived last night, and I must admit today I was keen to get out onto the headland as soon as I could. I thought my mother was sounding unusually nervy last night when I spoke to her."

"Well, things aren't looking good, it's only natural that she should be anxious. Hopefully she will be safe enough in her residential home, these things spread on public transport…overcrowded trains and buses have a lot to answer for."

"Thanks Stanley, I think I'd better catch up on the news."

I was too late; I tuned in to a regional news programme to find that traffic between the Balearics and mainland Spain had already been stopped. The following morning, the Spanish government declared a state of national lockdown, with residents only being allowed to leave their homes to buy essential food and collect prescriptions.

Within a few days, the novelty of unaccustomed peace and quiet was beginning to pall. My post retirement vacation was turning into a prison sentence and the prospect of being confined to one small room in the heat of summer was not an attractive one. I was glad of being able to exchange a few words with Stanley as I returned from the bakery.

"Ana, how's your mother, have you spoken to her today?"

"No, I phoned her a couple of days ago; she sounded fine, although she's having to spend more time in her room because the home is short staffed."

"I hope she'll be alright…the reports about COVID deaths in Madrid are pretty alarming, and the official figures are probably a massive understatement."

"I'm sure she'll be fine. Mum has her own room, she's doesn't need a lot of close contact personal care and she's never had any chest problems; even if she catches the virus, she'll probably just shrug it off in a couple of days. I'll give her another call when I get in."

"I think you should; I'm a bit worried about my brother back in the UK, the one with COPD. I think Boris is making a statement later this afternoon and everyone's expecting some sort of lockdown there too."

"It's inevitable I suppose, virtually the whole of Europe is under restrictions."

"Well, I might see you again in the morning if I need more bread."

"Look after yourself Stanley; you've got my number if you need anything haven't you?"

"Yes, thank you Ana. Give my best wishes to your mother."

I keyed in the number of the residential home in Madrid, but was met with a continuous engaged tone. After countless attempts, I gave up, and resolved to try again early in the morning, when the reception staff would be starting their shift.

"Buenos dias, Residencia Santa Maria."

"Buenos dias, quiero hablar con Susan Valdes."

"Lo siento, no entiendo," came the answer in halting Spanish. I was surprised, but tried again in English, wondering if I was speaking to one of the immigrant carers.

"I would like to speak to Susan Valdes, I'm her daughter, Ana."

"I'm sorry, I am new here. Many staff absent, sick. Wait a moment please."

I waited impatiently, for the first time starting to feel concerned about the situation in the home.

"I am afraid your mother is not well. Please call back tomorrow."

"But, what's wrong with her? Why can't I speak to her? She was fine at the week end."

"I'm sorry, we cannot take the phone to isolation rooms. She has chest infection and high temperature. I have to go now, please call back tomorrow."

The line went dead. I felt weak as a wave of anxiety struck me; for the first time I started to worry about the effect of the virus on my mother. I had never known her to have a chest infection; given the news from Madrid, the likeliest explanation seemed to be that she had caught COVID 19. I decided to call again in the afternoon, hoping that there would have been a change of shift on the reception desk.

I looked out of the window; it was a gloriously sunny day, which jarred with my miserable outlook. Not for the first time I regretted that the bakery was so close and that my quick trip to buy bread would be the limit of my time outdoors for the day.

Promptly at 2 o' clock, I called the Residencia Santa Maria. The receptionist who answered was a girl I had spoken to many times over the years, but her usual cheerful greeting had been replaced with a harassed and nervous tone as she spoke to me rapidly in Spanish. The news was not good; my mother had died at lunchtime.

I found some solace in the isolation imposed by the lockdown. There could be no family funeral, merely a cremation organised by the authorities in Madrid. At some point, they would send me my mother's ashes.

Over the following days, the situation in Spain appeared to be slowly improving as the strict lockdown curtailed the spread of the virus. In contrast, in the UK, the death toll continued to mount and there too, the impact on care home residents was severe. As I flicked through the TV channels one Sunday evening, I saw that the Queen was to address the nation and I duly tuned in to watch on the BBC News Channel. Her Majesty was smartly dressed in bright green, and closed her address with the words:

"We will be with our friends again; we will be with our families again; we will meet again."

The echo from the war years was poignant but how different the current situation was. For the first time, tears came, endless and exhausting as I felt overwhelmed by loss and isolation.

Two weeks later, I opened the shutters to the sound of shouts and laughter in the street below. Children were allowed outside to exercise for the first time and were revelling in their new found freedom. The doorbell rang; surprised, I hurried to answer it, glad of the opportunity to speak to another person face to face. The postman presented me with a small box bearing an official postmark. After chatting for a few minutes, I returned inside to open the package; it contained my mother's ashes. What would I do with them? Standing by the window, I looked across the road to the opposite balcony and glimpsed one of the residents tuning a guitar. He sat down beside the window and started to play, a haunting, lyrical piece by Albeniz, which seemed to encapsulate the essence of Spain. I had the answer to my problem; as soon as lockdown was over, I would go to my parents' favourite beach to scatter the ashes.

We will meet again.

# HOME SCHOOL

*May 2020, West Lancashire*

Alice stepped out onto the patio, breathing in the warm early morning sunshine, then pulled the French door behind her to escape the thuds coming from the lounge. The children were avid followers of the Joe Wicks morning exercises.

Her phone started to ring. "Hi Jo," she answered. "Not working?"

"Fat chance! I've been looking at spreadsheets for the past two hours and needed a break. It's amazing how much you can get done when you don't have to waste time commuting."

"You're not missing the office then?"

"Well, I do miss the company and I'm not keen on all these on-line meetings; it's difficult to tell what people are thinking. But I was really phoning to see how your first day back went."

"It was pretty strange. I suppose I should have been used to the queuing from the supermarkets but we don't normally get that at Homebase. The queue stretched right around the car park all afternoon and we were only allowing a couple of dozen customers into the store at a time. I saw loads of people I knew though; it seems like everyone has got a gardening project or a decorating project on the go."

"Not surprising if you're on furlough and only allowed out once a day."

"If you can afford it; I'm glad to be back on full pay even though it's going to be tricky juggling shifts and home schooling."

"I thought Gareth was taking care of that?"

"Well, he was, but now he's trying to get take away deliveries going to make a bit of money."

"Mum…" Alice heard a loud crash from the lounge, followed by the sound of her younger son crying. "Sorry Jo, I'll have to go. Sounds like World War 3's starting in the house!"

"No worries, I need to get on with a few VAT returns. Speak soon."

"Bye."

Alice stepped back inside, walked through the dining area and into the lounge. The TV was switched up to full volume and she swiftly reached for the remote controller to mute it. The two boys who were play wrestling on the floor got up abruptly.

"That's quite enough. School bags NOW," Alice said sternly.

"But Dan took my…"

"I don't care what Dan took, it's time to get on with your Maths. Your Dad needs a bit of peace and quiet to do the food orders." Alice glanced anxiously upwards as her husband's office was over the lounge.

"Sorry Mum, "said Max, sensitive to the tone of his mother's voice. At the age of ten he had learned that there were times when it was better not to argue. He would find a way of retrieving his Pokemon cards later in the day.

The two boys settled themselves at the dining room table. Alice helped each of them in turn with their Maths work sheets. After a mid-morning snack, she booted up her lap top so that Max could do some research for his history project on World War I and started to help Dan with a topic sheet about plagues.

"Can we go to Eyam to see the Boundary Stone Mum?" asked Dan after reading about the courageous efforts of the villagers. They had tried to prevent the Black Death from spreading by having provisions delivered to the outskirts of the village and leaving coins in payment in holes in the stone.

"Well, we could go to the Peak District for a day out once we're allowed to travel again."

"It's so boring being stuck indoors," said Max. "I want to play football with Olly and Joe."

"I'm sure it won't be too long before you're back at school again," replied Alice.

"Why do we have to be living in the middle of a pandemic, it's not like plague times when they didn't have proper hospitals and stuff."

"There have been pandemics before, Max. There was actually one during World War I, it was called Spanish flu. I think they might even have closed theatres and cinemas to try to stop people mixing; here, let me see what I can find on the computer." Alice reached over and found a history site which gave a brief summary of the impact of Spanish flu, which spread rapidly around the globe even whilst the war continued.

"Do you need to do anything else on your topic this week?"

"Miss Hawkes said we could look for soldiers' graves if we go for a walk in the churchyard, and also to look at the War Memorial to see if there are soldiers with the same surname who might have been brothers or cousins."

"OK, well this afternoon we can walk along the canal and then down to St Mary's church. That'll make a change. I seem to remember there are some war graves there, and then tomorrow, when Dad takes you into the village, you can look at the War Memorial."

"I suppose," said Max without much enthusiasm. It all sounded a bit dull compared to being able to play with his mates.

After lunch, Alice, Max and Dan set off along the tow path. A few people were out walking, enjoying the warm late spring sunshine. A familiar figure came jogging towards them.

"Hi Jo, fancy seeing you," said Alice.

Jo stopped a good two metres short of the family group. "It's a bit warm for running at this time of day, but it gives me a break.

This is my "It's not parkrun" five kilometres; I'm trying to keep my times up so I'm ready for when we can do the real thing again."

"Can I do parkrun with you, Mum?" asked Dan.

"Yes, I think you probably could manage it later this year," Alice replied, and turning to Jo continued, "If you could email me the route, I could try it with the boys at the week-end. I guess your circuit might be a bit easier than the course at Kew Woods?"

"Probably, it's all flat, so a good one to start with for Dan. Keep well away from the bank, though!" And with a cheery wave, Jo continued her run.

Alice and the boys took the next turning onto a public footpath which led along the side of a field of wheat and up to the main road. St Mary's Church was set back a little way from the road, surrounded by its graveyard; it was a traditional English village church, built of sandstone with a square tower and slate tiled nave. The church and graveyard dated back to the fifteenth century but Alice led the boys to the far side of the graveyard where the graves from more recent times were situated. It was remarkably quiet and peaceful; no planes overhead and even now, far less traffic on the roads than usual.

The boys darted about, reading inscriptions. Alice was helping Max to decipher names on a family tombstone dating from the 1900s when they were interrupted by a shout from Dan,

"I've found Grandpa's name! Come and look."

Max ran over to join his brother and started to read from the tombstone,

> "In loving memory of Emily Ainscough, born 3rd October 1900, died 12th January 1919. And of Frederick Ainscough, born 14th April 1880, died 30th April 1936 and of his wife, Elizabeth, born 21st July 1881, died 30th January 1970."

"See, I told you, that's Grandpa," persisted Dan.

"Don't be stupid. That Frederick was born over 100 years ago, and Grandpa's still alive," replied Max.

"It could be Grandpa's Grandpa, or even Great Grandpa," intervened Alice. "It used to be traditional to call the oldest son in a family the same name as their father. You and Dad could both have been Fred instead of Gareth and Max."

"Ugh…no way."

"Well, you'll have to phone Grandpa when we get home and see what he can remember about his family. How sad that Emily was only 18 when she died…and her parents were so young too. I'll just write these names and dates down, while you finish copying the names of the two soldiers." Max crossed back to the two war graves whilst Dan mooched along the row of gravestones.

"I can't find any more Ainscoughs, Mum."

"I think Grandpa's family mostly lived in Maghull and not in our village, so that may be why. Anyway, we'll have plenty to ask him when we get home."

Alice was pleased with the unexpected results of their afternoon walk. It had provided the boys with several new topics of conversation to replace the grumbling about the current lack of all forms of football. Replays of old matches did not really interest them.

"Hello, Grandpa?"

"Hello Max, how nice to hear from you. What have you been up to today?"

"I'm doing a project about World War I and Mum took us out on a walk to St Mary's. We found the grave of Frederick and Elizabeth Ainscough. Dan thought it was yours!"

"Well. I'm still alive, so you're not talking to a ghost!" Grandpa chuckled. "Frederick and Elizabeth were my grandparents, but I never knew Fred, he died before I was even born."

"So, Emily would have been your aunt?"

"Yes, that's right Max. She caught the Spanish flu from her fiancé. He'd been in the trenches for years, never suffered any injuries and then went down with 'flu as he was coming home."

"Oh…that's sad. Would you like to speak to Mum now?"

"Hi Fred, are you and Maureen OK?"

"Yes, we're fine. I was just telling Max about my aunt Emily whose grave you found this afternoon."

"It sounds like a sad story. I don't suppose you can remember the name of her fiancé?"

"Yes, it was Stanley Rimmer. His name is listed on the War Memorial in the village, although I'm not sure where he's buried."

"Well, that will be something for the boys to look out for when Gareth takes them out tomorrow. Now, do you need anything from Homebase? I'm working again now."

"A few more bedding plants wouldn't go amiss. At least the garden keeps us busy."

"Hopefully not too much longer before things go back to normal. I'll drop them off later in the week. Let us know if you think of anything else."

"Yes, I'll check with Maureen. 'Bye for now."

Alice turned as she heard Gareth coming downstairs.

"Were you just speaking to Dad?"

"Yes, Max was telling him about finding some of your family graves, Frederick and Elizabeth Ainscough and their daughter Emily. It's a bit of a sad story, she caught Spanish flu from her fiancé, Stanley Rimmer, when he came home at the end of the War, and they both died."

"I think I can remember my grandfather telling me about that, years ago. "

"Your Dad said that Stanley's name is on the War Memorial, so I thought you could find it when you take the boys out for a walk tomorrow."

"OK...is there anything else you need for your project, Max?"

"We have to write a story about what it might have been like to be a soldier..."

"Well, let's see if we can find out a bit more about Stanley and that might help to start you off. We can discover how old he was from the War Memorial and then we might be able to track down something on the Forces' war records web site about where he fought."

"That should keep you all busy while I'm at work! How about a barbecue tonight while the weather's good?"

"Yes please Mum," came the swift reply as the boys disappeared off into the garden to play football.


Three weeks later, Alice was standing outside the school gates.

"Hi Laura, back to the old routine."

"Yes, not for long though is it? And I've still got my older two at home, no sign of secondary schools going back in this term."

"No, that must be hard. It's bad enough with my two being in on alternate days. At least our lot will get their visits to the High School and the chance to get their bearings while it's quiet. I've had quite enough of supervising projects and worksheets."

"Hmm...the Year 6 stuff was pretty straightforward compared to Year 8 Maths. I can't remember doing anything that complicated when I was at school."

"I'll have to send for my friend Jo if we're still home-schooling next term. I really hope not, the kids have missed so much already. And it won't be the same for the Year 6s, going off to secondary school without all the usual treats. Max was so disappointed about missing the end of term trip."

"Jess was more upset about not having a prom, but I can't say I'm not relieved at being able to avoid buying a prom outfit and all the trimmings."

"Look, here they come…"

A few children emerged from the class room, which opened directly on to the Junior playground. In order to avoid crowding, parents had been asked to arrive at five-minute intervals. Max spotted Alice and ran towards her, with a wide grin on his face.

"Looks like you've had a good day."

"Yes, the best. We had loads of outdoor games and we didn't have to queue behind all the Infants at lunch time. And.." he paused for effect, "Miss Hawkes said my story about Stanley and Emily was an "excellent piece of original research" and I can be Team Captain for Sports afternoon next week."

"We'd better 'phone Grandpa when we get home and you can thank him for setting you off in the right direction. See you tomorrow, Laura."

"Yes, see you, Alice. Now Jess, how did **you** get on with the History project?"

"Miss Hawkes said all my work was very neat, but the story wasn't very imaginative," Jess tailed off lamely.

Alice couldn't resist a smile as she and Max headed home.

# DAY TRIP

*June 2020, Stoke-on-Trent and Formby, Merseyside*

Priya sank down onto the sofa and reached for the remote controller for the TV; finally, the children had settled for the evening. She was looking forward to the latest Jamie Oliver programme with its handy hints for food swaps and using seasonal produce, but her peace was short lived.

"Dad, come and say good night to us," called out Ravi, as he heard the sound of Amit's key in the lock. Priya stood up wearily, crossed the lounge and tip toed into the children's bedroom. Her son was looking expectantly towards the door, whilst his younger sister remained soundly asleep.

"Ssh, Ravi, don't wake your sister. Dad will come in as soon as he's washed his hands." Right on cue, Amit put his head round the bedroom door, "Had a good day mate? I hope you haven't worn your mum out playing football again. See you in the morning."

He kissed both of his children lightly on the head before retreating to the hallway.

"You look as tired as I feel. Something smells good, I'm starving."

He followed Priya into the kitchen where she was lifting his bowl of chicken biryani out of the oven.

"It really has felt like a very long day. The children don't get as tired as when they're at school and we're so short of space. It's not easy to get Ravi interested in the topic work school have sent home."

"Haven't you been out to the park?"

"Yes, but they're bored with that. Jasmin won't play football and Ravi's getting too big for all the apparatus. They've got too much time with just each other and they're missing their friends."

"Hopefully they'll be back at school before too much longer. But how about a day out tomorrow; we don't have to stay close to home."

"Where were you thinking of? It would be lovely to go to Prestatyn or Llandudno but we're still not allowed into Wales."

"There must be other seaside places. How about Blackpool?"

"So much will still be closed and it's quite a way. Is there anywhere nearer in that direction?"

Ravi was scrolling through Google Maps on his phone. "How about Southport, or wait, even nearer, Formby? It looks as if there's a long stretch of beach, but not much in the way of facilities. Perfect for a cheap day out."

"Here, let me look...well, that seems OK. Let's have an early night and surprise the kids in the morning. They can catch up on their worksheets at the week-end."

The kitchen was already flooded with bright sunlight when Priya got up at 7 am the following morning; it looked as if it would be yet another fine, warm day. She had packed a substantial picnic lunch before Ravi burst into the kitchen.

"Mum, can I...?" He stopped mid-sentence, looking confused. "Are we going somewhere?"

"Yes, your Dad's just checking the tyres on the car as we've not driven further than Tesco for months. We're going to have a day on the beach, somewhere new we haven't been to before. Does that sound better than Maths worksheets and football in the park?"

"YES! No work sheets today," he exclaimed in excitement. Then, after a slight hesitation, he asked, "Is it far?"

"Probably about an hour on the motorway if there's not too much traffic. Now, go and see if you can find your swimming trunks and a beach towel before breakfast."

Priya set Jasmin the task of hunting out last summer's buckets and spades from the hall cupboard whilst she checked off everything that they would need for the day. "Sun hats, suncream lotion, picnic lunch, water, wipes, beach towels, swimming kit, buckets and spades, travel rug."

"We're only going for a day, not a week," joked Amit as he came back into the flat.

"Well, it's best to avoid the shops so I want to make sure we don't forget anything."

"True, now let's have some breakfast and get going."

By 10 o' clock they were approaching the end of the M57 and had seen the first signposts for Southport, Ormskirk and Formby. There was an ominous file of red brake lights in front of them.

"There must be lights up ahead. I wonder where all this traffic's heading for," Priya said.

"Hopefully they're going to Southport, there must be a lot more to do there," replied Amit.

"I hope you're right. We're still going to be in this queue for a while though."

The queue of vehicles edged slowly forwards and the family were disappointed to find that the traffic was still queueing beyond the lights at the end of the motorway, and along the new link road to the A565 to Southport. Twenty minutes later, they finally reached a roundabout with a turning to Formby. Priya looked at Google Maps:

"It looks as if there's a National Trust car park fairly close to the beach. If you turn left at the next roundabout, we just follow the road straight on, over a level crossing and then it's about another mile."

A couple of minutes later, they found themselves in another queue of vehicles, struggling to make their way along a leafy residential road with cars parked on both sides.

"I don't think we're going to get to the car park…"

"Do you think all these people are going to the beach?"

"Well, it looks like it…see over there?"

Amit pointed to two cars which had pulled onto the kerb; the occupants were getting out laden down with beach bags. He turned into a side road. "I don't think it's worth wasting time trying to get closer, let's just park and walk."

"Are you sure?"

"Mum, I'm really hot and my tummy hurts," wailed Jasmin from the back seat.

"I think we'd better get the kids out into the fresh air; we can take it slowly going down to the beach. Hold on…"

Amit wound down his window as an elderly lady beckoned to them from her driveway.

"Are you looking for somewhere to park?"

"Well, yes…"

"You're more than welcome to park on my drive. I'm not going anywhere today."

"That's very kind of you."

"Have you come far?"

"Not that far … well, Stoke-on-Trent actually."

"Goodness, I haven't been further than Southport since lockdown started in March."

The woman took a step backwards, keeping her distance from the family as they climbed out of the car and collected their belongings together.

"I hope you have a lovely day." And with that she retreated back through the side gate of her bungalow.

"That was a stroke of luck. It's saved us a lot of hassle trying to find a space, and we're not too far from that road to the National Trust car park," said Amit.

"Are you OK Jasmin?" asked Priya anxiously.

"Can I have a drink of water?"

"Yes, of course; if we all have a drink now, that will be one bottle less to carry."

Amit checked that the car was locked and the family headed off towards the road to the beach.

Half an hour later, the family was installed on the beach, mid-way between the sand dunes and the water's edge.

"Can I have a sandwich Mum?" asked Ravi.

"It isn't even twelve o' clock yet. How about an apple to keep you going and then a paddle? I think the tide's going out, so I'd rather you went into the sea before lunch."

"But..."

"Your Mum's right. Hurry up and eat that apple and then let your Mum put some sun tan lotion on you before we go down to the sea."

"Can't you help me build a castle Dad?" Jasmin asked plaintively

"I'll help you with that Jas, and look, there's lots of shells here that you can decorate it with," coaxed Priya. Amit and Ravi raced off down the beach to the sea and Priya started digging out the outline of a sandcastle. Jasmin soon became absorbed in making smaller castles and arranging shells neatly around the sides. Priya looked up and down the beach; the sand stretched for miles in each direction. Beyond the menacing ranks of wind turbines, she could see the Welsh coastline to the south and the hills rising up in the distance; there was hardly a breeze and the sea sparkled in the sunlight. Breathing in the clean, warm air Priya almost forgot how tired she was after the weeks of isolation and home schooling, cooped up with the children in their small flat.

She looked down towards the sea and tried to picked out Ravi and Amit, amongst the increasing numbers of people paddling in the shallow water. Finally, she spotted them, daring each other to venture further into the water; she waved and eventually Amit waved back. Then he seemed to shout something, and started pointing; whatever was wrong?

"Jasmin, look, wave to Dad and…" Priya turned back towards the sandcastle and halted mid- sentence. There was no sign of Jasmin. Priya stood up and started to shout her daughter's name as Ravi and Amit ran back up the beach towards her.

"What a day to come back to work," said Anna as she surveyed the beach from the lifeguard's platform.

"Busiest one so far, it's going to be a scorcher," replied her colleague, Julian. "Better than being on furlough though, you can come down to the beach and get paid for doing it."

"I suppose you're right. I don't think I've ever seen so many people down here this early on a week day though. How many do you think will need pulling out of the water today?"

Julian surveyed the shore line before replying. "Possibly not that many, the sea's still pretty cold. Look, most of the kids are just jumping the waves."

"Well, I expect a few will get lost then."

As if on cue, a handsome Indian man in black swimming trunks approached the steps to their platform.

"Excuse me, I'm looking for my daughter…. she's small with black hair and a red swimsuit," he gasped.

"Where did you last see her?" asked Julian, standing up and climbing down the steps to Amit.

"My wife's sitting over there, about half way down the beach," Amit pointed. "My daughter was playing in the sand. Look, you can see her sandcastles. Her name's Jasmin and she's only five. We've never been here before and it's just so crowded."

"Calm down, sir, I'm sure she can't have gone far. We've got a good view up and down the beach from the platform," replied Julian reassuringly.

Anna was standing up, scanning the beach through a pair of binoculars.

"Hang on, has she got a pink bucket and spade? There's a little girl on her own just over there to the left," Anna pointed towards a small shape, which was crouched over and looking intently at something on the sand.

"Yes, yes, can you see her?" Amit scrambled up the stairs and almost snatched the binoculars out of Anna's hands.

"That's her; she must be collecting shells. Thank you so much." And he ran off as quickly as he had come to retrieve his daughter.

"Jasmin," he shouted. "What do you think you're doing?"

Jasmin looked up, startled by her father's angry voice.

"I was only collecting more shells."

"You went off without telling Mum, and anything could have happened to you."

"But, Mum was tired with building and I just wanted a few more shells."

"Never mind what you wanted. You really shouldn't have gone off on your own. Now let's get back to Mum and Ravi."

Jasmin's eyes filled with tears as she really did not understand what she had done that was so wrong. She struggled to keep quiet as her father marched her swiftly back along the beach, firmly grasping her hand.

"Jasmin, don't you ever go off on your own like that again," Priya admonished her when father and daughter arrived back at the family's base.

"It's a good job the life guards were on duty, they spotted her straight away," said Amit. "I really don't know how you could have let her wander off so far without noticing."

"I'm sorry, I was just looking at the view, and then waving to you and Ravi," Priya replied lamely.

"Mum, can we have lunch now, I'm starving," piped up Ravi.

"Yes, yes, I suppose so," said Priya wearily and started to unpack the picnic bag.

The family ate in virtual silence. After lunch, Ravi encouraged Jasmin to finish building her castle whilst Amit went for a swim. Priya didn't take her eyes off the children for a second.

"I think we ought to start packing up now," said Amit when he returned. "I don't want to spend hours in a queue to get back to the M57."

"But Dad, it's only 2 o' clock," started Ravi, but quickly fell silent again when he caught sight of his father's expression.

Moira stood back and surveyed her two freshly planted containers. The petunias looked quite small but with regular watering and a bit of plant food, they should provide a colourful display for several months. She looked around in surprise as she heard footsteps on the drive.

"Hello, you're back early; are you going home already?"

"Er, yes, we want to avoid the queues getting back to the motorway," replied the Indian man curtly.

"Mum, I need a wee," wailed the little girl.

"Shh, Jasmin, let's get the car packed. Ravi, put a dry T shirt on please."

"But Mum, I can't hold on."

"Why don't you come and use my toilet while your Dad and brother get the car packed," Moira offered, without thinking.

"Really, we couldn't..."

"Mum, I really, really need a wee now." The little girl started to cry.

The husband and wife exchanged glances, and the husband nodded.

"That's so kind of you. If you're really sure…"

"Yes, my bathroom is just opposite the front door, across the hall," Moira replied, as she led them up the path to the bungalow and opened the porch and front doors wide. "You just go ahead, and I'll wait out here for you."

Within a couple of minutes, mother and daughter emerged back onto the driveway. "Thank you so much, that was very kind of you. We won't have to stop at a service station now."

The family quickly got into the car and Moira waved as they drove off towards the main road.

"Had some visitors, have you?"

Moira turned as her neighbour walked down his path.

"No, of course not Bill, no one's allowed visitors at the moment. The family were looking for somewhere to park and I offered them my drive."

"I thought I saw someone coming out from your porch though."

"I just let the little girl use my toilet, she was desperate poor thing. It's so difficult when there are no proper facilities at the beach."

"Really, Moira, I'm surprised at you. What if they've got COVID? We're at a very vulnerable age you know, we really shouldn't be mixing at all. I was only saying to Ken at the golf course," he hesitated before continuing, "Well, there's nothing wrong with a round of golf in the fresh air."

Moira smiled wryly as Ken retreated to his bungalow. Her visitors would give him and Brenda something to talk about for days. She returned inside, sprayed disinfectant onto her bathroom sink, bleached the toilet and opened the window.

"I never, ever want to go to Formby again," said Priya as Amit turned off the M6 and onto the Stoke ring road.

"It was a lot more crowded than I was expecting, and a lot further to walk" replied Amit. "But at least the kids have worn themselves out." Both Jasmin and Ravi had been fast asleep for the last hour.

"Yes, if it hadn't been for that old lady, Jasmin would have been hysterical by the time we got to the first service station. That really would have been the final straw. But I hope our next trip's to North Wales; somewhere with shops, toilets and car parks near the beach."

"Shall we pick up some fish and chips on the way home?"

"Good idea."

# THE LAST SISTER

*August 2020, North Devon*

"Now, take a deep breath, and as you breathe out, start to roll down slowly, one vertebra at a time … "

The shrill and unexpected ringing of the landline interrupted my online Pilates session. I stood up abruptly.

"Hello, could I speak to Andrew Brown, it's Eileen from Co-Op Funeral Services." The caller sounded brisk and efficient.

"I'm sorry, I'm afraid he's out. Can I take a message?" I replied.

"Well, we've got a funeral booked in for St Stephen's, 11am next Friday. I know it's short notice, but the family were quite insistent; the deceased is Angela Lerwill."

My mind was racing, trying to make connections. Lerwill, the name was familiar, one of the oldest families in the village, judging by the number of headstones in the churchyard dating back over four centuries. I had no idea who Angela was though.

"OK, I'll pass the details on to Andrew and ask him to call you back later. As you know (well, she must know, or she wouldn't be calling Andrew), the vicar's in hospital and we'll have to find someone to take the service. It won't be easy."

"I'll leave it with you, but please make sure Andrew gets back to me no later than 3.30pm because the office is only open for reduced hours at the moment."

With that Eileen ended the call. I stood staring at the receiver, still half raised to my face. Here we were, in the middle of a global pandemic, and these undertakers could only think about their own convenience; did no one realise that Church Wardens are volunteers?

My husband had been hoping to relinquish his position as Church Warden of St Stephen's in April, but COVID and lockdown had put paid to those ideas. Now, in August, life was starting to return to normal, but our vicar had been in hospital for weeks in an induced coma after contracting COVID in the spring.

I heard the front door closing as Andrew returned from his morning run.

"Bad news, I'm afraid," I greeted him. "The Co-op have called, they've booked a funeral with us for next Friday."

"But I've told them, we can only take funerals on Wednesdays or Thursdays so that the building can be closed for 72 hours before the Sunday service…"

"She was insistent, it's a member of the Lerwill family … "

"Hmmm…well, we don't want a load of grief on Brancoombe Broadcasts for upsetting local worthies. I'd better see if Tom Martin can take the service."

He retreated to the bathroom to shower and change. I returned to the lounge to find that my Pilates class had finished. I searched for Brancoombe Broadcasts on Facebook to see if I could find out any more about Angela Lerwill. Sure enough, there was an entry in the News section:

### Angela Lerwill, last of the Brancoombe Lerwills

Angela Lerwill, last surviving daughter of John and Ethel Lerwill, died peacefully at home on 31$^{st}$ July, aged 94. The Lerwill family contributed significantly to the development of Brancoombe when the opening of the railway line from Barnstaple to Ilfracombe brought hundreds of tourists to the area. Wilfred Lerwill, a renowned cabinet maker, endowed Brancoombe Grammar School in the 1880s and other members of the family contributed significantly to the building of the new chancel in St Stephen's Church. Whilst most members of the family have left the area, Angela spent all her life here, working a smallholding in the hamlet of Dunton. She preferred animals to people and homes are now being sought for her five tabby cats. All enquiries to Brancoombe Broadcasts. A private funeral service will be held at St Stephen's church at 11am on 12$^{th}$ August.

Not much privacy there then, although it sounded as if Angela herself had been a somewhat eccentric and reclusive lady. However, not every elderly spinster's death merited a write up in the local "press" and no doubt there would be plenty of people with time on their hands to come out to line the streets for a view of more illustrious members of the family...and we hadn't even accepted the funeral booking yet. I resolved not to mention this snippet to Andrew.

*****************************************

The following Friday was a typical English summer's day: warm, with sunny spells and a gentle breeze. St Stephen's nestled in the middle of its large graveyard, a squat limestone building with a square tower. I had found myself cast in the role of honorary verger as we were still anxious to protect our normal team, all in their 80s, from contact with strangers.

Inside, the church looked very much as it may have done in the late nineteenth century, in the heyday of patronage by the Lerwill family. Modern song books, the recently purchased pew Bibles in contemporary English and brightly coloured Welcome Cards had all been removed. Alternate pews had been roped off to ensure that members of the congregation remained socially distanced. I just had time to hoover the bright blue carpet (prone to showing up every speck of dust) before the arrival of Rev Tom, a retired priest who had settled in Brancoombe.

"I think it would be best if you stayed in the vestry until the coffin is brought in," suggested Andrew, keen to ensure that Tom remained at least two metres away from the mourners throughout the proceedings.

"No, Andrew, that simply wouldn't be right," retorted Rev Tom. "I must greet the family at the gate when they arrive, and reassure them before they come into church."

"Well, OK, but let's ask the undertakers to pause at the doorway to allow you time to walk up the aisle and take your position at the lectern before they follow you."

"Yes, that would work, but how will we manage the end of the service?"

"You could leave first through the vestry; the coffin bearers will proceed down the main aisle as usual, followed by the mourners. That'll give you time to walk over to the grave before them. I'll feel much happier once you're out in the open air."

"Right, I'll get my robes on and wait at the gate. I assume you and Susan here will look after the undertakers, sort out the music and so on."

Andrew suppressed a grimace; he was becoming increasingly irritated by the idiosyncratic ways of undertakers.

"Yes; they've already brought over the CD with all the music for the service, and we've set out the orders of service in the pews so that people will know where to sit. Sue's got a sheet to record details for "Track and Trace" and we'll make sure no more than thirty people come into church."

"Good, it looks like you've got everything under control. I should just mention that all six of Angela's great nephews and nieces will be contributing to the eulogy section of the service."

"But...." Andrew was left expostulating as Rev Tom disappeared into the vestry. "I can't have six of them up at the front with Tom. Goodness knows how many of them could be asymptomatic. I'm not going to be responsible for killing anyone in this congregation."

"Calm down, dear," I said. "Look, just put one of the spare microphones at the foot of the Chancel steps and the family members can speak from there. It'll be less intimidating for them."

I went to take up position outside the church door with my clipboard. Beyond the churchyard, on the pavement, small groups of people had assembled. I hoped they realised we could only allow thirty mourners into the building, and weren't going to complain to Brancoombe Broadcasts when they were turned away; although, to be fair, the funeral announcement had clearly stated that this was to be a private service.

My fears proved to be groundless; only twenty mourners approached the entrance to the church before the limousine arrived, transporting the six great nephews and nieces. Full marks to the undertakers for their preparations.

Half an hour later, there was still no sign of the service ending. I glimpsed through the open doorway.

"We used to love staying with Aunt Angela, she made such fantastic cakes."

"We would help Aunt Angela feed the hens. They were the best holidays of my life."

"Aunt Angela was a staunch Devonian, she will be greatly missed by all her friends at the Women's Institute."

… and so it went on, the unending platitudes of a guilty family who probably hadn't seen their spinster aunt for years. My train of thought was interrupted by the sound of heels clicking on the church path.

"I take it this is where the funeral of Angela Lerwill is being held," demanded the new arrival, a tall well-groomed woman in her late 50s, wearing a smartly tailored floral dress and a pink fascinator, more appropriate for a wedding than a funeral.

"Yes, but the service is nearly over, it started at 11.30," I replied, but my words went unheard as the woman had already walked straight past me into the church. It was a good job we hadn't already reached the attendance limit.

Five minutes later, Rev Tom emerged from the vicar's vestry and walked swiftly over to the freshly dug grave. I stood to one side as the coffin bearers came out of the church, followed by the family. After a short pause, the woman in the pink fascinator appeared, paused to look over toward the grave and strode off briskly down the path. I retreated into the church to help Andrew; all the pews would have to be thoroughly wiped down with anti-bacterial spray, given that it was less than forty- eight hours to the Sunday service. Andrew was looking in a bemused way at an envelope.

"Is that a donation for the Cats' Protection League?" I asked.

"Er, no, I don't think so. That woman who arrived late gave it to me, she asked if I was the Church Warden."

"Well, you'd better open it."

Andrew carefully opened the thick cream envelope and drew out a closely written card:

"To the current Church Wardens of St Stephen's, Brancoombe.

I wish to advise you that my late mother, Angela Lerwill, has bequeathed her estate in equal shares to St Stephen's Church, Brancoombe, and St Stephen's Primary School, Brancoombe. Her will is deposited with Colclough and Gordon Solicitors, of Barnstaple.

Thank you for arranging the funeral service in these difficult circumstances.

Yours

Annette Lerwill."

Andrew had turned white. "Do you think it's a hoax? No one

has ever mentioned a daughter. Angela Lerwill's small holding in Dunton could be worth several hundred thousand with Planning Permission; that amount of money would solve all our problems with the leaking roof..."

"I think we may need to arrange an appointment with Adam Colclough, but it sounds like good news. Just now though, I really need a spot of lunch after such a long morning. How about going to the Mason's Arms?"

"Good idea, you go on ahead and I'll lock up when Tom's written up the Register. It's just a pity it's not earlier in the week and we could have had a free lunch from the Chancellor with "Eat Out to Help Out. I knew there was a good reason not to have funerals on Fridays."

## SEPTEMBER MORNING

Bright sunshine on a September morning
*Saylyn* berthed at a tranquil mooring
Bacon sizzling in the galley kitchen
A mug of tea before departing

No need to fear
I am alone

The barge glides smoothly forwards, ropes pulled in
Down the canal, bordered by trees
Leaves still green but red berries are gleaming,
Conkers are falling, the glossiest brown

No need to fear
Here all is well

A blue flash between reeds; a kingfisher
Dives, swoops upwards again; ducks paddle away
I stand idly watching, warmed by the sun
The scenes that repeat week after week

No need to fear
Life will go on

Mid- morning coffee and chocolate biscuits

HILLARY GRIFFIN

Approaching a village, people appear
I wave to joggers, greet mid- week walkers
Perched at the helm, socially distanced

No need to fear
Watching from here

White washed cottages alongside the path
A large tabby cat asleep in the shade
Gardens bright with red pelargoniums
Wrought iron chairs facing the water

No need to fear
Away from the crowd

I see the next bridge, with steps down to the path
A woman descends, pulls off her mask
Harassed and haggard, shoulders hunched forwards
She inhales deeply, I see her relax

No need to fear
Now home at last

# RACE AGAINST TIME

*November 2020, West Lancashire*

"No, I'm sorry Jess, I won't be taking on any temporary staff over the Christmas period."

There was a silence as the caller hesitated before replying.

"But I thought you would be opening up again as the lockdown will be over at the end of the month, and I'll be coming home from Uni that week."

"I'm afraid I'll be continuing on a take-away only basis; maybe a café style service during the day time but I can manage that myself. It just isn't economic for me to re hire evening staff when everything's so uncertain, especially as October was a disaster with the Tier 3 restrictions. But I know where to find you next year and hopefully we'll be back to normal in the summer."

"OK, thanks Gareth."

"Bye Jess."

Gareth sighed as he ended the call. He really didn't like having to turn staff away, especially the students who worked hard and happily accepted whatever shifts he offered them.

"Who was that?" his wife, Alice, asked as she came into the spare bedroom that had now become a home office.

"Jess Rimmer, asking for work at Christmas. I had to tell her I wouldn't be opening the restaurant in December."

"So, you've made your mind up?"

"Yes, I've run through the figures to see what's viable as tables are still likely to be restricted to six. And do you seriously think the usual groups of over 60s will be going out for lunch?"

"But some people may be glad to go out for a meal after a month of lockdown."

"I'm not convinced and I don't want to take the risk. I can save on staffing and heating costs, and just concentrate on the cake and dessert orders, plus take away drinks. The food for the Christmas menus is pricy and we can't afford to end up giving best sirloin steak and outdoor reared turkeys to the Food Bank."

"OK, if you're sure. Would you like me to ask Jo to cast an eye over your figures before we make a final decision…just in case she has any bright ideas?"

"Well, I guess it wouldn't hurt if she's not too busy. I can't afford her firm's fees though; you'll have to see if she'll do it as a favour."

"I'm sure she will. I get the impression her workload's dropped a bit; people are putting off accountancy work as long as they can to save costs."

Alice's mobile pinged.

"Oh no, that's all I need," sighed Alice.

"What?"

"It's Max's school. The whole of Year 7 are being sent home for ten days because they've picked up some positive COVID cases on this morning's testing."

"Does that mean he'll have to self- isolate?"

"I guess so; I'll have to move Dan's stuff into here so that Max can have the bedroom to himself. I'll set my laptop up in there so he can do his school work online."

"Just keep him away from me. We may not be getting many orders, but I still need to be able to do deliveries."

"I could ask for a couple of weeks' furlough."

"We could do with your money at the moment; but it might make things a bit easier with Max being at home. Yes, go ahead, see if your supervisor will allow it."

The front door slammed.

"And here he is, right on cue."

Alice returned downstairs to greet her eldest son.

"Hi Mum, did you get the message, we've all got to self- isolate, Josh Brown and Nathan Cartwright have got COVID. They were sent to an isolation room while the rest of us packed up all our stuff."

"Yes, and I'm afraid you're going to be packed off up to your room, well away from your Dad."

"But…"

"Sorry mate. You can have my laptop to do your school work and Dan will have to sleep in the office."

"YES! A room to myself. And do I get to keep the Playstation?"

"I suppose so. Come on, let's get you sorted."

Alice spent the rest of the day reorganising her work and thinking through the logistics of keeping Max isolated from the rest of the family in a three bedroomed terraced house with one bathroom. She was relieved that the rain had stopped in time for her to walk to the local primary school to collect her younger son.

"Had a good day, Dan?"

"Yes, we had outdoor games this afternoon. I'm starving, what's for tea?"

"Bangers and mash"

"Great, and then Beavers."

"No, there's no Beavers tonight, your meetings have been cancelled because of the lockdown."

"But I was going to finish my Skills Challenge, it's all I've got left to do before I go up to Cubs."

"Well, maybe Rusty Beaver will message me to let me know what you've still got left to do and we can sort it out at home. She didn't forget you all during the first lockdown."

Dan trudged on quietly, his good mood blighted by the disappointment of Beavers being cancelled. When they arrived home, he spotted Max's school shoes and coat in the hall.

"Why's Max home?"

"Oh, I'm sorry, I forgot to say. Two of his class have tested positive for COVID so they've all been sent home. He's got to self-isolate, so you'll have to sleep in the office until he's allowed out again."

"But that's so not fair. It's really poky in there."

"Well, you only need to go in there to sleep. Max has got to stay in one room all day and do his school work in the bedroom too. Your Dad's working in the office a lot, so Max can't sleep in there."

"But what happens if I get COVID?"

Alice was spared having to answer that question by the arrival of an email from Rusty Beaver. She skimmed through it quickly before answering Dan.

"Here we go, Rusty Beaver's given me a few ideas about activities to finish off your Skills Challenge. And there's another challenge on the Scout website, it's about raising money by walking and running during lockdown. You add up your miles and log them onto a map. Let's go and have a look at this on Dad's laptop."

Dan had already started rushing up the stairs before Alice had finished speaking.

"Ssh… Dan, I'm just on the phone to Alex sorting out an order."

"Go on Alex, you need eggs, plain flour, vanilla bean paste, glace cherries, lemons and walnuts. OK, I'll go to the wholesaler's first thing before opening up for take aways. See you in the morning."

Gareth put the phone down.

"Look Dan, you really need to remember that this is my office at the moment. I could have been in the middle of taking a big order from a customer."

Alice caught up with Dan and frowned at her husband; the boys had been remarkably well behaved and uncomplaining as they had scrimped their way through the last few difficult months.

"Anyway, have you had a good day at school?"

"Yes, but Mum's going to show me something from Rusty Beaver."

"Great, come on let's have a look."

Together, father and son opened the link to the new "Race Around the World" section of the Scout Association website.

"Let's see. So, there are four teams: Beavers, Cubs, Scouts and Explorers. Rusty Beaver is going to register your Beavers and add your miles into the Beaver Team total. If we look at that map, the race has already started; the Cub Team is half way across the Atlantic, but Beavers aren't far behind. And to help the Beavers, Mums and Dads can walk or run too and add their miles on to yours."

"How many miles do you think we could do this month?"

"Well, if you walk to school and back every day, that's two miles plus an extra four for Mum and me because we're going there and back twice. Say twenty days at six miles, so 120 altogether. Between us I'm sure we could manage 20 miles at the week-ends so how about a target of 200? We can ask Nan and Gramps to sponsor you and Mum could ask some of her choir buddies."

"We'd better hope for plenty of dry weather, it won't be much fun walking to school in the rain," remarked Alice. "But if we walk, the miles will soon tot up and we'll save on petrol."

"What about Max?"

"Max will have to wait until his ten days' isolation are up, I'm afraid."

"Can I phone Gramps and ask him to sponsor me? And will you ask Jo?"

"Yes, OK. Now let's go and get the tea started."

*****************************

The weather was remarkably clement for the following week and the family had already accumulated over fifty miles for Race Around the World thanks to both Alice and Gareth completing five mile runs at the week-end.

On a dull Monday afternoon, Gareth reviewed his spreadsheets yet again, and finally plucked up the courage to call Jo.

"Hi Jo, it's Gareth, sorry to bother you, is this a good time?"

"Oh hi, Gareth. It's fine, I'm not too busy today. How's the takeaway business going?"

"To be honest, it's not been great so far this month. People aren't so keen on sitting out on park benches in the middle of November to drink a cup of takeaway coffee. We're still doing a reasonable number of dessert orders but the margin's barely enough to cover Alex's wages."

"It sounds tough. I guess you're not entitled to claim any government help. There's been a lot of press coverage about the plight of directors of small companies."

"There's relief from Business Rates and the VAT reduction for hospitality, but I've still got to pay the rent. We didn't do too badly over the summer, but just now I can't see any end in sight."

"Jo mentioned you'd decided not to re- open the restaurant in December."

"No, it's hard to see trade picking up at the end of lockdown when the groups that can meet together socially will be so restricted. I mean, we're not going to get the usual round of pensioner lunches, let alone office Christmas parties."

"The youngsters may be desperate to get out and socialise but you're probably right about the older generation."

"Anyway, the reason I was calling was to see if you'd mind taking a look through my figures, just in case I've missed anything. I may need to approach the bank for a short- term loan."

"OK, no problem, email them over to me. Hang on, there's some breaking news on the radio…"

There was a pause as Jo turned up her radio. "Wow, they've just announced that Pfizer have run successful trials for a COVID vaccine."

"That could be a gamechanger; a vaccine's the only realistic way out of this nightmare. I don't think this lockdown is having the impact the government hoped for."

"Let's hope it'll be approved quickly. I can't begin to imagine how the NHS will cope with vaccinating the whole population though."

"Or how long it will take … I just hope they start with the elderly. Mum and Dad have put a brave face on being isolated but it's tough for them to have seen so little of the kids. I'm not sure what we'll do at Christmas. Either of the boys could be unwitting carriers when they have so many contacts at school, and Dad's chest isn't good. Still, that's a problem for another day. I need to check on Max, he's on the last day of his self-isolation. I'll send you over the spreadsheets, let me know what you think."

Max returned to school the following day, and Alice was able to end her furlough leave and return to work.

**Three weeks later**

Alice pulled the car onto the short driveway in front of their house; no sooner had she stopped than the boys scrambled out and ran to knock on the front door.

"Dad, we ran two miles through the pinewoods."

"Well done, all that way without stopping?"

"Yes, Dan slowed down but he kept going."

"Great stuff, go and get a shower and change out of your running kit before you catch cold." The two boys kicked off their trainers and headed off upstairs. Alice was leafing through a bundle of letters that the postman had handed to her.

"This looks like one from the bank, I thought we'd only just had a statement?"

She passed the envelope to Gareth, who looked a little sheepish. "I think I know what it might be," he started as he pulled out the letter and skimmed through the contents.

"I applied for a short- term loan, and the bank have agreed; it's just to cover the rent for the next six months."

"But…I thought you said you didn't want to take on any more debt?"

"Yes, but I need to be realistic. I spoke to Jo and ran through my forecasts up to the end of March on the basis that there wouldn't be any significant improvement in trading compared to the beginning of November."

"Surely Christmas will be better now we're out of lockdown?"

"It may be a bit better, but then we could be back into lockdown again in January, especially as this new Kent variant is spreading like wildfire and it's going to take time to vaccinate everyone. And don't forget, January's always a poor month when people have splashed out on Christmas. A loan makes more sense than an emergency overdraft."

"How will we pay it back?"

"Keep our fingers crossed that the restaurant will be open as normal in the summer. Jo suggested keeping my restaurant prices unchanged and not passing on the VAT reduction to customers; she reckons the majority of hospitality businesses will be doing that to make up for losses over the winter. She was really helpful. It was good to have a chat with someone independent who understands business."

"So, my choir membership has had some benefits then?" Alice asked archly.

"Yes, I suppose it has. And I'm sorry I didn't mention the loan application before; it's been a strange couple of weeks, with Max at home and you working evening shifts."

"Well don't make a habit of it. I'd rather know how bad things are with the business sooner rather than later ... "

"Mum, can I..." Max stopped as he sensed the tension between his parents.

"What is it?" asked Alice sharply.

"I just wanted a glass of water."

"Yes, OK, you must be parched after all that running. Sorry mate, I didn't mean to snap."

"Is everything alright Dad?" Max asked as Alice left the room.

"Yes, all sorted. Come on, let's go and check what football's on today, isn't there an early kick off? And then we'll need to get ready to go and see Dan get his Beaver badges."

After a well- earned round of bacon sandwiches, the family set off to the Scout Hut. Rusty Beaver, a short, bustling woman in her mid- fifties, had organised a family treasure hunt. Each family group had to follow a trail around the grounds and answer questions designed to test every age group at ten marked boards. Gareth had agreed to provide take away hot chocolate and gingerbread biscuits at cost price.

When the families had completed the trail, they stood along the driveway in their socially distanced groups to await the presentations.

"Hi Alice, it's turned a bit chilly."

Alice turned towards the next family group, which included Oliver, from Dan's class, and his competitive mother, Kate.

"Oh, hello Kate," replied Alice.

"This hot chocolate's great, is it on Gareth's take away menu?"

"Yes, and the biscuits are a special for December." Alice paused, searching for something else to say. "Is Oliver looking forward to Cubs too?"

"Definitely, he's started to get a bit bored with Beavers to be honest, although goodness knows how long it will be before Cub meetings start."

"Oh look, Rusty Beaver's about to start the presentations," replied Alice, relieved to end the conversation.

The family groups moved apart again as Rusty Beaver put her hand up for silence.

"Hello again everyone and thank you all for coming. I'll try to keep this short as it's starting to get cold, but I have some really special news after we've found out who's won the quiz. Akela's handed around the answer sheets and we'll trust you to mark your own sheets. Has everyone checked their answers? There were 30 points available, have any families scored over twenty?"

"Shh Dan, I'm counting…" hissed Max and then shot his hand into the air. Most families had scored over twenty.

"21…22…23…24…25."  Only three hands remained raised, including Max's.

"26." Another hand was lowered.

"27."

"That's our score, look Oliver's won AGAIN." Dan muttered, glaring across the drive at Oliver's family.

"Well done to the Blundell family with a winning score of 29. If you'd like to come and collect your prize from the table."

Oliver smirked at Dan and marched up to the table to collect a large tub of Heroes.

"And now, the results of our Race Around the World sponsorship. With the grand total of 210 family miles, the clear winners are the Ainscough family. Dan, would you like to come forward to collect badges for your family."

Dan skipped delightedly up to the front and Rusty Beaver pointed at a small plastic bag, which contained three "Team Beaver" badges.

"And if you'd like to stay there a minute Dan," whispered Rusty Beaver. She turned back to the rest of the gathering. "We would normally have a special presentation evening for our Beavers when they move on to Cubs, but sadly we can't do this at the moment. But I'm delighted to say that Dan has also completed his Chief Scout Bronze Award and will be moving up to Cubs when we restart next year. So, Dan, if you'd like to pick up that bag," she pointed to another small plastic bag containing a smart hexagonal bronze badge with the Scout emblem, "let's give Dan a round of applause."

Alice felt a lump in her throat as Dan returned to his place in the family group; another milestone in the children's lives had been reached.

"Thank you so much Rusty Beaver, Dan's loved his time in Beavers."

"He's done well to finish his badgework on his own, none of the others have. I'm not sure what will be happening next term, but I'm sure Akela will be in touch."

"Anyway, have a good Christmas in the meantime. Bye."

The families dispersed back to the car park. Alice spotted Kate trying to console Oliver who was complaining bitterly about not receiving a Chief Scout Bronze Award badge. She was glad now that she had encouraged Dan to persevere with his badge work at home.

"Can I phone Gramps and tell him about my badges? Do you think you can sew both of them onto my Cub sweatshirt?" asked Dan.

"Yes, of course you can phone Gramps once we're back home in the warm. We'll take some photos of your badges too and put them on the family WhatsApp group."

When they arrived back at the house, the landline was ringing.

Alice picked it up,

"Hello Maureen, the boys were just going to call you. Dan's ... "

"Sorry Alice, I need to speak to Gareth, Fred's been taken to hospital."

Gareth snatched the phone from Alice. "Mum, what's going on?"

"I had to send for the ambulance, your Dad's had a bad chest all week but today he was really gasping for breath. The ambulance men were so kind, but they said he ought to go into hospital to be properly checked over. And no one's allowed to go with him."

"Has he taken his mobile phone?"

"Yes, but I don't know if he'll be allowed to use it."

"OK, don't worry. I'll try to call him and then I'll get in touch with the hospital and see what I can find out."

"Thank you."

"Just have a word with the boys while you're on, and I'll call you back as soon as I've got any news."

Gareth passed the phone to Dan, who immediately started to tell Maureen about their afternoon at the Beaver treasure trail and his new badges. Gareth dialled his father's mobile but there was no answer. He disappeared up to the office to start trying to call the hospital.

"Come on boys, give me a hand to get tea started so that we can all watch Strictly together."

"Is Gramps going to be alright?" asked Max in a worried voice.

"Yes, I'm sure he'll perk up once he's got the right medicine. I expect you'll be able to speak to him later," replied Alice as brightly as she could.

It was over a half an hour before Gareth came down and beckoned Alice into the kitchen.

"What's wrong?"

"He's in the process of being admitted to a ward so that they can give him intravenous antibiotics. They want to do chest X-Rays too. We'll be able to speak to him later."

"So, it's nothing more serious than an infection? It's not unusual for your Dad to have a chest infection at some point in the winter."

"I know, but we've all been so careful around him and now he's somewhere that's far less safe for him than being at home."

"But if he needs antibiotics … "

"Yes, he has to have them. I just wish he'd had a COVID vaccination."

Two days later Gareth took the call he had been dreading. Fred had tested positive for COVID and he and Maureen were asked to visit the hospital to say good-bye for the last time.

# THE RED COAT

*December 2020, Liverpool*

A blast of Mersey chilled air funnelled up Hanover Street as Stella hurried out of Central Station on a grey Monday morning in mid-December. She pulled on her gloves and walked briskly up Church Street to Debenhams, an imposing modern building situated in a commanding position on the corner of South John Street and Lord Street. The windows were covered with details of clearance sales and final reductions; a sad reminder of the uncertain future facing the department store, once a darling of the High Street.

"Hi Stella."

Stella turned towards the young woman who had followed her through the doors.

"Morning Laura. Are you back with us for the holidays?"

"Yes, I've just got shifts for the three weeks until New Year. I started yesterday; there's bargains on all the women's wear, and the perfumes. I can't wait to go round with my Staff Discount Card."

"I might have a look later. The sales might bring a few more people in, but it's not been too busy so far this month, you wouldn't think we'd been closed for the whole of November. Anyway, you know the ropes after being with us last summer."

"I'm just glad to be coming out to work and the pay's not bad here. I really don't mind where I end up after spending most of the last term cooped up in a student hall."

"No, I'm sure it's not what you thought it would be like when you applied for Uni."

"I'm glad I wasn't too far away from home and some of my mates were in the same hall, so at least we could eat together sometimes.

How've you been getting on?"

"Well, we've been able to open the church again for Mass and I've been helping out with the sides person's duties. A lot of the older members of the congregation who would normally do that still aren't happy to go out. I'm shopping for a couple of them too."

"Are you able to sing? I love Christmas carols and Nativity plays."

"I'm afraid we can only listen to recorded music. Singing's just too risky; I think some people are singing behind their masks though. It does all feel really strange. Anyway, enough of this, I've got to go down to the Personnel office before opening time."

"Surely you haven't done anything wrong?" Laura looked at me aghast.

"No, nothing like that; it's actually my last day. I'm retiring at the end of the month and I've got to use up my annual leave."

"Oh, what a shame we can't have a party for you, give you a proper send off. But you'd better make the most of your Staff Discount Card, especially with all these bargains around."

"Yes, hopefully I'll have time later on."

The two women went their separate ways. Stella had taken up her customary position on the main payment counter on the Womenswear Floor well before opening time. A trickle of customers wandered around, homing in on the bargain rails in each section.

"Excuse me, could you just check the price on this coat for me?" asked a middle aged woman, approaching the counter with a short red pea coat. "Is there really another 25% off on top of the first reduction?"

Stella scanned the barcode.

"Yes, that's right, the price now is £37.50."

"I'd have been happy to pay £50, but now I can have the T-shirts for that price as well."

"It's certainly a good day for bargains."

Stella carefully folded the coat and two T shirts.

"Would you like a bag Madam?"

"No, I've actually brought one with me. I had to go into the Post Office with some documents to send by recorded delivery. The queues were right round the floor, and people were standing far too close together. I haven't felt frightened like that before; half of them weren't wearing their masks properly, you'd think people would have learned by now."

Stella, straightened her mask self-consciously to make sure it was firmly over her nose. "I'm sorry to hear that. At least there's plenty of space in here so you don't need to stand too close to anyone. Are you paying by card?"

"Yes, of course."

"If you could just pop your card into the machine and enter your PIN number. There, that's all gone through, you can take your card out now."

"Thank you. I'm glad I came in here. I haven't been shopping for clothes for months and I certainly won't be coming back into the City Centre until I've had my vaccinations. I hope you're still open then."

With that, she turned and headed towards the escalator. Stella thought to herself that she certainly wouldn't be there when the woman next ventured into the City Centre. Even the presence of the store itself was in doubt after yet another potential investor had pulled out of negotiations to take over the remains of the Debenhams portfolio.

A few minutes later a man in his sixties approached the counter. He too was carrying a red pea coat; Stella looked again and realised he had two coats in his arms.

"Excuse me, is it possible to return items that have been in the sale?" he asked nervously, looking rather uncomfortable.

"Yes, certainly Sir, provided that you return them within fourteen days."

"Thank you; I'll certainly be able to return the one I don't want before then. I'm sorry, I'm not being very clear. I'm buying them for my mother and I'm not quite sure which size would be best. She's been shielding for months but I need to encourage her to go out to get her vaccination done. I thought a new coat might buck her up a bit."

"That's not a problem at all Sir. Would you like a bag?" replied Stella as she took the coats from him and started to fold them. They really were very good value.

"Er ... yes, please. And I'm paying by card."

"There you are Sir, that'll be £75. If you could just pop your card into the card reader. There, that's all gone through for you. I hope your mother likes the coat and that one of them is a good fit."

"Thank you very much for your help."

He, too, turned and headed off to the escalator.

The number of customers gradually increased during the morning and Stella served a steady flow of bargain hunters. She was glad when it was time for an early lunch break, and spotted Laura sitting on her own in the staff room.

"How's your first morning been?" Stella asked.

"Ugh, I'd forgotten how boring it is trying to look busy when no one really wants you to help them. I must have tidied the jumper display three times already."

"Which section are you on?"

"Principles."

"Their coats have been selling well this morning. I think I've packed up half a dozen and I'm sure Karen's sold some too."

"Everyone loves a bargain and you don't really expect them until after Christmas. Anyway, I've been asking round the girls and we can't let you go without some sort of send off. Just make sure you're here for afternoon tea break at four."

"I hope you're not planning a party, there's all sorts of rules about that."

"I know, I know. Don't worry, I've already checked with Personnel. I'd better get back to the jumpers before the floor manager spots that I'm missing."

"I'll see you later then."

Stella finished her sandwich and returned to her counter. It was busier during the early afternoon as the bargains lured city centre workers into the store. Shortly after three o' clock, there was a lull and Stella's colleague, Karen, urged her to take a look around for some bargains while she still had the benefit of her Staff Discount Card.

Stella remembered the pea coats that she had sold earlier; the coat was just the right length to wear with trousers and she knew that the red was a shade which would suit her. She made a beeline for the coat rail in the Principles section and found the pea coats. She rummaged along the rail, but there was only one red coat, in a size 8, far too small for her. She turned sadly to the display of jumpers that Laura had carefully arranged and picked out a couple of items.

Half an hour later, Stella duly made her way to the Staff Room and was greeted by a round of applause from her colleagues who were standing around the edge of the room, all still wearing their masks and carefully keeping their distance from each other.

The personnel manager stepped forward:

"Well Stella, as I'm sure you know, this isn't how we would have planned to celebrate your retirement and I'm sure you'll appreciate that a staff party is against all the social distancing rules, but Laura here persuaded me that we couldn't just leave these gifts on the counter at the end of the day. So, here you are, with our thanks for your hard work over…how many years is it?"

"Just the one year here, but fifty years in Southport before that."

The personnel manager looked a little askance, she clearly wasn't up to speed with Stella's employment history. "You must have seen a lot of changes over the years, but I don't expect you expected to retire in the middle of a pandemic," she continued hastily, trying to gloss over her lack of preparation.

"Thank you all so much. I really didn't expect anything, particularly the way things are at the moment," replied Stella.

Right on cue, Laura stepped forward with a large tray of cup-cakes, topped with swirls of garish pink icing, which she offered around the room. One of the other temporary girls followed her with a tray of glasses of something sparkling, which turned out to be grape juice.

The conversations were a little stilted under the watchful eye of the personnel manager and Stella was relieved when people started to drift back to their counters. As she was returning to the cash counter, Stella took one last look at the coat rail in the Principles section: she could scarcely believe her luck, when she saw a red pea coat in her size. She quickly grabbed it and paid, using her Staff Discount card for the last time.

At 5.30 pm her shift ended and she headed for the exit; given the question mark over the company's future and rumours of further lockdowns in the New Year, she wondered if it would be for the last time ever.

Lord Street was busier now and Stella had to weave between the crowds as she hurried to Central Station. She was quite laden down with her own purchases and the bags containing her retirement gifts. In the entrance to the station precinct, she bumped into a man, hurrying in from the opposite side of the road and the shock made her drop one of the bags.

"I'm so sorry, I wasn't looking where I was going," he said, in a voice that sounded vaguely familiar.

Stella was scrambling to gather her new clothes back into the carrier bags, but as she straightened up, she realised where she had seen the man before.

"Thank you, that's very kind."

"Wait, didn't you serve me at Debenhams this morning?"

"I think ... yes, were you buying coats for your mother?"

"Yes, and I can see you've bought one too."

Stella was slightly embarrassed and unsure how to reply, but the man was still speaking, "And I brought one of them back later on because it was too small."

"That was lucky for me because there wasn't one in my size on the rail at lunch time but when I checked later on, I found this. It should have been quarantined for 72 hours but the temporary staff probably didn't realise. There are so many new rules at the moment."

"Well, I'm glad."

"I must rush, I don't want to miss my train," Stella replied, wondering how she was going to get away.

"Good bye, then."

Stella rushed down to the ticket barriers, clicked her pass on the automatic gate and hurried on to the escalator for the Northern Line. The platform had been crowded but when the train pulled in, she was relieved to find a seat at the back of a carriage. She was stowing her bags beside her, unaware that another passenger had sat down opposite; she looked up to see the same man again.

"I'm sorry, I really wasn't following you," he said bashfully. "I live in Crosby."

"What a small world, I'm from Waterloo," Stella replied.

They chatted tentatively to each other for the next twenty minutes and Stella found herself warming to this rather gentle man, whose name was John, and telling him about her strange retirement day.

As the train approached Waterloo, John said,

"It's been lovely to chat to you. Do you ever walk up the Promenade past the Iron Men?"

"Yes, if the weather's good, I often go out for a walk on Sunday afternoons."

"I might just bump into you again then," he said and then somewhat hesitantly added, "If that's OK?"

Stella smiled at him. "Yes, of course," she replied.

# THE DRIVE IN

*December 2020, North Devon*

"At last, a free morning to do the Christmas shopping; are you sure you wouldn't like to come into Exeter with me?" I asked my husband playfully, knowing full well that even a committee meeting on Zoom would be preferable to a December shopping trip, especially after another month of lockdown.

"Quite sure thank you, dear. I don't know why you can't just order all the presents on Amazon, you wouldn't even have to spend time wrapping them up, let alone queue in the Post Office … "

"After four weeks of tramping to and fro along the Coastal Path, walking round the Guildhall Shopping Centre has a certain appeal. I'm just hoping there'll be somewhere to sit down and have a bite to eat at lunch time."

"Have you totally taken leave of your senses? COVID hasn't gone away just because Boris has allowed the shops to open again. The Treasury needs the Christmas VAT receipts, so never mind the pressure on the NHS…"

"Oh Andrew, stop being so miserable. I'll make sure I sit at least two metres from anyone else and choose a well-ventilated spot. If the sun comes out, I might even get a take away and sit on a park bench…again. And while I'm there, I thought I'd look round one of those bargain Christmas outlets to see if I can pick up a few more decorations for the Christmas Activity Afternoon."

"Hmm…well, people are supposed to bring their own decorations, to avoid handling anything from outside their own household. If you're going to start doling stuff out, it's one more thing to add to the Risk Assessment."

"Don't worry dear, I may not even find anything suitable, and I'll update the Risk Assessment if necessary."

I picked up my car keys and headed out. It was a relief to be able to escape from Brancoombe after the last lockdown and a few hours' Christmas shopping seemed like a real treat rather than a tedious chore. So many of the usual Christmas activities would be out of the question this year with the COVID restrictions in place: no carol concerts, no Nativity plays, no Christmas parties. The traditional Wreathing Afternoon when the interior of St Stephen's Church was decorated with wreaths made by small groups followed by tea and mince pies had had to be replaced. In its place, we had organised an outdoor activity where families could come to decorate small Christmas trees which had been carefully spaced out around the boundary of the churchyard. Bring your own decorations and Thermos flasks! Still, it would be better than nothing.

As I drove along the A377 towards Exeter, weak gleams of December sunlight broke through the clouds and my spirits lifted as the sky brightened. The school holidays had not yet begun and I was able to find a parking spot close to the town centre without too much difficulty.

By lunch-time I had completed all my shopping, and was particularly pleased with the selection of angel and star decorations that I had found in one of the "pop-up" Christmas shops; these could be distributed to the family groups at the Christmas tree decorating afternoon, to give a finishing touch to each tree. Each individual decoration would need to be bagged a few days' beforehand to eliminate the risk of spreading infection. I had also found some large bottles of hand sanitiser at a bargain price; presumably everyone had stocked up so much earlier in the year that sales had dried up. Even Andrew couldn't find too much to complain about with all these precautions in place.

It was so mild that I opted for an outdoor picnic lunch and picked up a turkey and cranberry roll and a bottle of flavoured water in Marks & Spencer. I found an unoccupied bench close to the cathedral where I could sit and enjoy my lunch before heading home.

"Andrew, are you in?" I called as I opened the front door. "Shh...I'm in the middle of a Zoom meeting with the vicar and Maisie." Andrew poked his head around the door of the dining room where the laptop was set up beside an ominous looking pile of paperwork. Maisie was the newly appointed Church Warden, still full of enthusiasm for her role, whilst months of dealing with COVID restrictions had sapped Andrew's energies ... not that he had ever had much enthusiasm for Christingles and carols.

I retreated to the spare bedroom to hide the Christmas presents away.

Ten minutes later, the dining room door slammed and I heard the opening music of a film as Andrew switched on the TV. I knew better than to ask how the meeting had gone when I snuck in with tea and chocolate biscuits; I was sure that I would find out soon enough.

"So, did you have a successful shopping trip?" Andrew asked as we sat down to our Wednesday night tea of shepherd's pie and garden peas.

"Yes, I found presents for almost everyone on the list ...and a few extra decorations for next Saturday's event. I'll get them bagged up tonight and distribute them on the day, to minimise the risk of fomite transmission," I added cautiously.

"Next Saturday is the least of my worries after this afternoon's meeting. You'll never guess what the vicar wants to do on the Sunday before Christmas. We've only had one Sunday back in church since lockdown and already it's a nightmare convincing the sidespeople that they don't need to exchange a week's news in the entrance porch. They should just be concentrating on making sure people come in, fill the pews from the front and sit where there's an order of service. And then they complain about sitting in a draught, it's not exactly Arctic conditions at the moment; surely, it's not too much to put on an extra layer compared with the risk of catching COVID. In a few more months, we'll all be vaccinated and be able to go back to normal."

"And what is it exactly that the Vicar wants to do?" I interrupted, as Andrew paused to draw breath. "Surely he's happy with all the procedures you put in place during the summer when he was ill?"

"Oh, he's not bothered about any of that as long as he can run two services each Sunday. And then, on the Sunday before Christmas, he wants to have THREE."

"Three ... but surely there isn't time to fit in another service on Sunday morning, not when you need to ventilate the building and wipe down the pews between services?"

"Aah, well, it's not on Sunday morning. He wants a service of Carols by Candlelight at 6pm."

"But we aren't allowed to sing, how is that going to work?"

"Never mind about singing, how are we going to light candles? We can't be tripping up and down the aisle like we usually do ... passing people, handing out jam jars, sharing lighter s..."

"Well, no, I can see that ..."

"And of course, Maisie told him it was a wonderful idea and she would find some suitable recordings of professional singers for us all to watch."

"It may all come to nothing when they've had time to think it over. Let's get Saturday over with first. It's still another couple of weeks to Carols by Candlelight and things may have changed by then."

Andrew accepted my attempt at pacifying him and retreated to the lounge to resume watching his film while I washed up.

The mild weather continued for the rest of the week, and a good number of families assembled in the church yard to decorate trees on Saturday afternoon. Everyone had brought enough decorations for a tree, and dutifully sanitised their hands before selecting a bag with either a star or an angel from my box. I was sorry not to be able to join in with the decorating, but we couldn't allow different households to "mingle", even outdoors. The number of COVID cases in our area was heading upwards again, but a greater concern was the situation in the South East and my fears that our adult children would not be able to return for the Christmas break.

"Ah, Susan, another splendid effort," my day dreaming was interrupted by a loud, confident, male voice.

"Oh, hello Terry, I didn't expect to see you here," I replied. Terry Gibson was a leading light in the local rotary club, but not a regular member of St Stephen's congregation.

"I was just out for a walk, feeling at a bit of a loose end without the Santa's Sleigh to organise."

"I suppose that would be out of the question this year, house to house collections won't be allowed."

"No, and a lot of our members are still very nervous about mixing at all. I can't wait for the vaccination programme to start."

"Well, we will miss hearing your carols this year and the children will miss seeing Santa."

Terry wandered out through the churchyard and crossed the road to the large open air car park. I remembered bringing our children to see Santa's Sleigh when it finished its rounds back in the car park and played "We Wish You a Merry Christmas" to entertain the Christmas shoppers.

And then, I had one of those sudden flashes of inspiration, a real light bulb moment. Why not have a community drive in carol service? I was sure that Terry had recordings of carols as well as secular Christmas songs plus he had all the necessary electrical equipment. There was plenty of space in the car park, even if the cars had to be socially distanced! Maisie could organise bookings on Eventbrite. My mind was racing, but this really did seem as if it could be a substitute for the worrisome Carols by Candlelight.

My only dilemma was whether to speak to the vicar directly or broach the subject with Andrew first.

"Susan, are you ready to go home yet?" Andrew approached the lychgate where I had been stationed all afternoon.

"Yes, everyone is supposed to take anything home that they don't use, so there shouldn't be any clearing up to do."

"Well, at least that all went smoothly; dealing with the indoor events is another matter entirely."

"Actually Andrew, I've just had an idea about December 20$^{th}$ that might save you a few headaches."

"Hmmm … the vicar and Maisie are very set on Carols by Candlelight, COVID or no COVID"

"No listen, I've just been speaking to Terry Gibson from Brancoombe Rotary and he's really missing doing the Santa Sleigh rounds. So I thought, why not have a Drive In Community Carol Service in the car park, using the Rotary Club's equipment? Far more people could come than we can accommodate in church at the moment, so surely the vicar would be pleased? You could ask Maisie to set up a booking system, that would keep her busy."

"And nothing for me to do?"

"Well, you might need to marshal cars on the night … "

"I suppose I could manage that, as long as I'm not standing in the wind and rain for too long. You wouldn't want me to be laid up with 'flu when the children come home."

"I'm sure it will be a fine evening, don't be so pessimistic."

"And how long have you lived in North Devon … ?"

Amazingly it seemed remarkably easy to organise the Drive In service, which was greeted enthusiastically by all the churches in Brancoombe. As predicted, Maisie was delighted to put her IT skills to use organising a booking system. The vicar appeared relieved to be able to cancel the Carols by Candlelight service without having to admit that it was a little too risky an undertaking in the middle of a fresh wave of COVID infections. Even the weather was co-operating, with a change to colder, drier conditions forecast for the week-end.

On the Saturday before the Carol Service, I had just finished wrapping family Christmas presents when an announcement on the early evening news caught my attention.

"A new Tier 4 is to be introduced with immediate effect in the South East of England due to the rise in infections of a new COVID variant. It will be mandatory to "Stay at Home" and all non- essential retail, leisure facilities, and hospitality venues are to close. The rules previously announced relating to "Christmas bubbles" will not apply to Tier 4 and it will not be permitted to travel in or out of this area."

My heart sank, even though I should have been expecting this; yet again our hopes of seeing our children had been dashed.

"Susan, do you know where the camping light is? I'm not sure where I'll be standing tomorrow night and I've got to be able to check the car registrations off against Maisie's booking list." Andrew stopped mid- sentence when he saw the expression on my face.

"Whatever's the matter? You look dreadful."

"I feel dreadful."

"You're not running a temperature, are you? I told you not to go into Exeter, half the people you see in shops still don't know how to wear a mask properly."

"For goodness' sake Andrew, that was weeks ago. No, I've just heard the latest announcement about Tier 4 restrictions in the South East."

"Tier 4, what on earth's that?"

"Lockdown, effectively. No movement in or out, Stay at Home, shops closed, no socialising, Christmas cancelled for those of us with family in that over populated part of the country. James has been saying for weeks that restrictions should have been tighter in London."

"Are you sure you've got this right? Boris has only just announced the rules for Christmas."

"Well, you're the one who's been telling me that the virus doesn't stop for Christmas and the government shouldn't be trying to give people what they want," I retorted.

"Yes, I know, and they've been very slow to acknowledge the new variant. Still, it won't be too much longer before we get vaccinated and you can catch up with James and Ruth on Zoom without tiring yourself out with all that extra cooking and laundry."

"Christmas on Zoom, I've heard it all now. I thought you hated Zoom."

"Well, endless unnecessary meetings on Zoom … but it will be better than a phone call."

"Anyway, I've had enough, I'm going to have a large glass of red wine and watch *Strictly*," I snapped.

For once, it was Andrew's turn to withdraw and return with a conciliatory glass of Malbec.

I was still feeling miserable the following morning and refused to go with Andrew to the traditional service of Nine Lessons and Carols at St Stephen's, normally a highlight of the Christmas season. I really did not want the sympathy of friends whose children had settled in the South West and whose major worry would be working out their Christmas social bubbles. Andrew and I would be spending Christmas Day on our own for the first time in thirty years; at least the extra large Christmas pudding would keep in the cupboard for months.

I spent the morning out on the coastal path, enjoying walking in the brisk westerly wind.

"Are you still coming to the Drive In service this evening?" Andrew asked warily later that afternoon.

"Yes, I suppose so; we've got our ticket and you'll be able to sit in a warm car once everyone's arrived. With any luck, I won't have to discuss family Christmas arrangements with anyone else."

"It makes a change from me trying to avoid people who haven't been able to sit in their favourite pew or don't like the vicar's choice of carols."

"Who has chosen the music for this evening anyway?"

"Your friend Terry from the Rotary Club asked a selection of organisations to nominate something from the Bethlehem Carol Sheet; it's a compromise between making sure we had a consistent quality of recordings and getting people involved. He's really put a lot of effort into this and it's taken his mind off Santa's Sleigh."

"I'm glad about that."

The day had been clear and sunny, but the temperature was starting to drop sharply by the time we left for the Drive In just after 5pm. Doing my best to enter into the spirit of the occasion, I had packed a Thermos of hot chocolate and home baked mince pies into my bag.

The car park soon filled up with cars, carefully spaced out in alternate bays. From what I could manage to see, there was a good mix of families and older people. Many had followed the instructions to wear a Santa hat or at least something red. The whole area looked very festive with the Christmas lights switched on.

Terry was delighted to be announcing each carol, and I had to admit that the recordings were of a very good quality. I sat back and listened to the well known words.

"And now, chosen by St Stephen's Church, our final carol, "It came upon the midnight clear". A good choice for an evening event. Before we close, I would like to take this opportunity to thank Maisie Thomas for masterminding the ticketing of this event, and all our marshals for their help with directing you to your spaces this evening. We hope that you have all enjoyed our community event and that you will have a safe and healthy Christmas," Terry concluded.

My thoughts drifted, as the words of the carol sounded out; a very different Christmas marking the end of a year that none of us could have imagined the last time we sang this at St Stephen's at the beginning of the Midnight Communion Service.

"And those whose journey now is hard, whose hope is burning low,

Who tread the rocky path of life with painful steps and slow:

O listen to the news of love which makes the heavens ring!

O rest beside the weary road and hear the angels sing!"

# TAKE THREE DADS

*Scotland, December 2020*

Dusk was falling over the granite walled houses of suburban Aberdeen as another dreary December day drew to a close. Inside a neat semi-detached house, three middle aged men were sitting around a table, busily wrapping items in a selection of brightly coloured foil paper.

"Pass me the Sellotape, Malky, quick now, before I lose my grip on this fold," said the eldest of the trio, a thick set bearded chap, who was carefully holding down the flaps of gold foil paper around a small box.

"There you go, that's me done," replied Malky, showing off a beautifully wrapped purple parcel. "I see you've gone for the easy option Robbie," pointing at the third parcel, in a deep red gift bag.

"Aye, I can't manage all this fancy stuff. Do you want a brew before you go?" asked Robbie. "And Morag's made some mince pies too, with that whiskey mincemeat you like."

"No, I'll be getting along home, I don't want to spoil my tea and we've got an early start tomorrow. I guess we shouldn't really be doing this at all; I'm not sure you could argue that we're all in the same social bubble," replied Malky.

"Morag and I haven't been in close contact with anyone since lockdown ended so you'll not be catching COVID in this house."

"I've kept myself to myself too," added Charlie. "I won't be seeing anyone over Christmas either. Alastair thinks he'd be too much of a risk to me as there's so many COVID cases in the school at the moment. It's been really tough for teachers this term."

"So, what time are you picking us up tomorrow, Charlie?" asked Robbie.

"7.30 sharp. We mustn't be late as we need to be parked up at the Visitor Centre before it gets too busy."

The three men set off on schedule the next morning, the boot of Charlie's 4 by 4 loaded up with their back packs, walking sticks and hiking boots. As they approached the Visitor Centre at Bennachie, the sky was clearing and there was a hint of the sun breaking through the low clouds.

"Looks like we might be OK lads, although the forecast wasn't great," remarked Charlie.

"Don't speak too soon, remember the year when we had to spend a night out here in our bivi bags."

"How long ago would that be…10 years?"

"About that, it was one of our early walks, only a year or two after Laura passed"

The men fell silent, remembering the reason for this annual pilgrimage. Within the space of two years, all three had suffered the death of a teenage daughter: one suicide, one drug overdose and one road traffic accident. They found some solace walking the slopes of Bennachie; the exertion of the climb in winter was an antidote to sitting around at home watching Christmas trivia on T.V.

"Come on lads, it's a fine morning, who's got a song?" Robbie started them off with a burst of "Good King Wenceslas" in his booming voice, with Malky, a tenor, taking the part of the page.

An hour or so later, as they emerged from the oak woods which covered the lower slopes of the hillside, the sun had disappeared and the sky was looking ominously grey.

"Look, the crofter's selling teas." Charlie pointed to a large sign resting against the wall of a small croft house. "We'll get warmed up and then crack on."

As they turned onto the path leading to the croft, a squat building nestling into the hillside, a small red- haired woman came out.

"I'm sorry, I can't let you come inside…the First Minister's just banned all indoor hospitality."

"That woman! The power's gone to her head!" exploded Charlie.

"But I've got some picnic tables in the yard, and I can put the patio heater on for you," continued the woman.

"That would be great, we'll have three teas," said Robbie.

"And I expect a wee dram wouldn't go amiss, just for medicinal purposes," offered their hostess.

"No indeed," replied Malky.

Half an hour later, suitably fortified, the three men continued on their way, glad of the warming tot of whiskey as the temperature was already dropping noticeably. They crossed a section of open moorland and then headed onto a track into pine woods.

"What do you think, another half hour until we reach the chapel?" asked Malky.

"About that, if the weather holds," replied Charlie. At that moment, the first flakes of snow started to fall, and within seconds the visibility had deteriorated.

"At least we're on the track now … " started Robbie.

"But we won't be able to see it if the snow keeps coming down at this rate," finished Malky.

The three men struggled on. The snow had quickly covered the track and was falling even more heavily. After about quarter of an hour, they heard a noise, approaching from behind. They moved to the side and a battered Land Rover pulled in alongside them.

The driver wound down his window, lowered his face mask and shouted:

"Are you OK? Do you need a lift?"

"We're only going as far as St Nathalan's Chapel."

"I'm stopping at the croft just this side of it."

"A lift would be very welcome and save us some time, if you're sure you don't mind."

The three men pulled on face masks and piled into the vehicle. "Thanks for doing that. By the way, I'm the GP, I've been called out to a lady who's about to give birth," their driver explained.

Any further conversation was impossible as the old vehicle bumped noisily along the track.

After about ten minutes, a light loomed ahead of them, and they stopped outside a small log cabin. "I think it's a holiday home; they weren't expecting the baby to arrive for another couple of weeks," said the GP.

Alerted by the noise of the vehicle, a flustered looking man in his early thirties had come to stand in the doorway. "Am I glad to see you, the baby's arrived … "

The GP hurried into the cabin, leaving Charlie, Malky and Robbie in the Land Rover. "Shall we carry on?" asked Robbie.

"It seems a bit off to go without thanking him properly," started Charlie.

"Come on in and help me wet the baby's head," shouted the man from the doorway.

"Well, there's an offer we can't turn down," finished Malky.

The three men hurried into the cabin, still holding their backpacks. Inside, there was a roaring wood stove. The GP emerged from the bedroom holding a small bundle wrapped in a white shawl; the baby was sleeping peacefully, oblivious to the panic that her premature arrival had caused.

"We're only here for a few days, we never thought Sarah would go into labour," said the husband. "We were expecting a boy, but it's a girl. She seems to be healthy, so all's well."

"What are you going to call her?" asked Robbie.

"We hadn't chosen a girl's name."

"Laura", "Hannah", "Abigail". The three men spoke at once.

Their host looked taken aback by the chorus of voices.

"I'm sorry, it's just that we come up to the chapel every year to remember our daughters, they are very much on our minds today," explained Charlie. "But if you two don't mind, I think we should leave our presents here to welcome your new daughter."

"Great idea," replied Malky and from their back packs, the three men produced the gold wrapped box, the red gift bag and the purple parcel.

"Thank you, there's really no need…"

"It's our pleasure, "said Charlie firmly. "Far better for someone to benefit from our gifts rather than leaving them in an empty chapel."

Shortly afterwards, once the doctor had completed his checks on mother and baby, the four visitors left the cabin. The snowstorm had stopped as suddenly as it had started and the three men continued on their way to the chapel to pause for a while and rejoice at the wonder of a new birth.

# SPRING BLOOMS

### *March 2021, North Devon*

"Yes, Maisie, I'm more than happy for you to organise the cleaning." I heard Andrew's voice as I pulled off my coat and boots in the porch.

"No, it's just a normal thorough clean as the church hasn't been used since Alan Carter's funeral at the end of February. If you look at the Church of England guidance, it's very clear, we don't want to be using any cleaning materials that could damage the pews or kneelers. The main thing is not to leave it to the last minute, I'd like it all done at least a week before Easter in case the vicar decides to run any other services in Holy Week. Ideally, choose a fine day so that the cleaning team can work with all the doors open for ventilation."

There was another pause whilst the speaker replied.

"I'll see you at the PCC Zoom meeting tomorrow night. Bye for now."

Andrew turned to greet me, "Oh, hello Susan, is it that time already? I'm afraid I haven't got the tea on yet; the phone hasn't stopped ringing all afternoon. Life was so much easier a couple of months ago, when we just had to send out the Zoom login for church services."

"Don't worry, let's just have some soup and a bacon sandwich tonight. It's been a really busy session at the vaccination centre, no time to go inside to warm up. The wind rattles through that car park."

"Maybe it will be a bit quieter in April. The powers that be are forecasting a slowdown in the number of first- time vaccinations although they still seem confident of getting the over 50s done before May."

"That's all very well, but with Brancoombe's population, there'll be a lot of older folk due for their second vaccinations soon. At least the weather should be starting to warm up; it might be quite pleasant standing out in the sunshine."

"Right, I'll get the kettle on … "

As Andrew headed into the kitchen, the landline started to ring again.

"Oh, hello Susan, it's Linda Evans. Is Andrew around please? I just need to ask him about Easter flowers."

"Yes, Linda, hold on a moment, I'll go and find him for you."

I put my hand over the receiver as Andrew returned, mouthing "Is it for me?"

"Yes," I whispered. "Linda with a question about flowers."

Andrew rolled his eyes as he took the 'phone. "Hello, Linda, how are you doing?" After a lengthy pause, whilst the speaker fired off a volley of questions which I couldn't hear, Andrew replied in his most authoritative voice, "I'll just stop you there Linda. This really isn't "back to normal"; I will be telling the vicar that we need to keep everything very simple, just as we did after the previous lockdowns. There will be the **same** social distancing measures, hand sanitiser, masks, track and trace procedures and recorded music. There will be **no** notice sheets and **no** flowers."

The voice on the other end of the line did not sound pleased.

"Well, I'm afraid that's the way it is. There are plenty of spring flowers that people can enjoy in the safety of their gardens or out on their walks without the need for them in church. We can save the money we would have spent on Easter lilies. Goodness knows, we need to make a few economies at the moment."

Another angry reply followed. I did wish Andrew would be a little more diplomatic at times. No doubt I would be tasked with phoning Linda tomorrow to calm her down.

"Did you say something about a cup of tea?" I ventured.

"A stiff gin and tonic wouldn't go amiss. I've a good mind to ignore the phone and just deal with answer phone messages in the morning. Everyone else has a working day, I don't see why a church warden should be on call 24/7."

Before Andrew could carry out his threat, the phone rang yet again. I picked it up, anticipating another query from a church member with too little to do.

"Hello, Susan speaking."

"Hello Susan, it's Claire. I'm afraid I've got some bad news. Richard's been admitted to our local hospice, the cancer has spread far more quickly than the doctor thought."

"But...I was only speaking to him at the week end. He sounded quite upbeat."

"He's in a lot of pain now. I don't know how he's kept it from us all for so long."

"It's hard to tell on the phone, and I haven't seen him for months."

"Well, you're so far away from the rest of the family."

"How are Jenny and the children coping?"

"They're all pretty shocked, obviously. At least they're being allowed to visit. I doubt that either of us will see him again though." Claire's voice trembled; she and Richard had always been close whereas I saw very little of my siblings.

"I'll text Richard and see if he's able to speak to me. I don't want to disturb him when Jenny and the children are there," I replied.

"I'd better go. Jenny has asked me to contact Richard's work and a few old Uni friends."

"You will let me know if there's any change?"

"Yes, of course, bye for now." The line went dead and I sat down, stunned.

"Whatever's the matter?" asked Andrew.

"That was Claire, Richard's been admitted to the hospice. How did we not know he was so ill?" I couldn't hold the tears back any longer.

"Perhaps Claire's got it wrong, she does tend to overreact, maybe it's respite ... "

"No, Andrew, I really don't think so. Jenny's asked Claire to contact Richard's colleagues and close friends, she wants us all to be prepared."

"I'm sorry love ... "

I pulled myself together. "I must tell James and Ruth, Richard is James' godfather after all."

"You do that and I'll get the soup on."

I was very glad of a session at the vaccination centre the following day. It was routine administration work, checking off appointment times as members of the public arrived for their first dose of COVID vaccine. The weather had taken a turn for the better and it was pleasantly mild standing in the late March sunshine.

We had an early tea as Andrew had to prepare for yet another PCC meeting on Zoom. I had received one text from Richard saying he was feeling very tired but would try to call me later. I settled down to watch an old episode of Death in Paradise in peace whilst Andrew retreated to the study.

It was after 10pm when he finally emerged.

"Gosh, that was a long meeting."

"Hmph ... the vicar wanted two services on Easter Sunday. He thinks more people will want to come than we can accommodate in church with the social distancing rules."

"He's got a point. A lot of people will be desperate to get out of the house and they'll feel more confident after having their vaccinations. We had no services last Easter either," I reminded Andrew.

"I wasn't prepared to run two services so close together in the building, so the compromise is that there will be an early

Communion outside on the lawn. Maisie is going to organise a booking system for both services, and the later service will also be on Zoom."

"You'd better do a Parish email to let people know what their options are, you don't want to leave anyone out."

"Good idea, I'll sort it out in the morning. It's less than a fortnight away so there really isn't much time," sighed Andrew. "But now I'm off to bed."

My mobile phone beeped and I scrolled down to open a new text message:

"Richard passed away peacefully in his sleep at about 9pm. Speak to you tomorrow. Claire x"

I could scarcely take it in, and sat looking at the message. How could this have happened so quickly?

"Susan, you're not still watching that rubbish?" Andrew reappeared in the doorway to the lounge.

"Are you alright, whatever's happened?" His tone changed when he saw me.

"It's Richard; he's died, just in the last hour. I should have phoned, I haven't even seen him since last summer, and now I won't … " I sobbed.

"Come on, it's not your fault. With all the restrictions around shielding, and the lockdowns, how could you have visited?" Andrew tried to comfort me.

"You're right, of course. I need to let the children know."

"Look, leave it until the morning, and I'll do it. Let's not disturb them so late."

"I'll just have a mug of peppermint tea, that might help me to sleep."

"Well, don't sit up too long. We've all got a busy day tomorrow."

I went through the following day on autopilot; it was a relief to have the routine activity at the vaccination centre to occupy me. Andrew told our children about Richard's death, and I spoke briefly to my sister- in- law. I wondered about the funeral arrangements, and as I had heard nothing by the week-end, decided to contact Claire.

"Oh Susan, yes, I'd been meaning to speak to you. Jenny's almost finalised the arrangements. The funeral will be next Saturday, church service followed by burial."

I was surprised. "Easter Saturday? Are you sure?"

"Yes, there's a backlog up here and the undertakers were keen for the funeral to be held before Easter. As it's a burial rather than a cremation, Saturday was an option."

"It'll be a bit difficult for Andrew when he's got two services to sort out here on Easter Sunday, and I'm not sure what the train services will be like for the children … "

"Well, I was coming to that. The thing is, it's been really hard to allocate places for the funeral. Obviously, Jenny has had to invite some of Richard's colleagues and then there are the neighbours who have supported them through the last few months, and as you know, there's a strict limit of 30."

Claire paused and I could almost hear her taking a deep breath before continuing, "There are only two places for your family. I'm really sorry, but there'll be a Zoom link so that the James and Ruth can watch online."

"But, James was Richard's godson!" I exclaimed, then bit my tongue. The rules were the rules, as I knew only too well after witnessing Andrew's efforts to enforce them over the past year. "I'll speak to Andrew, but it may be that James comes to the funeral with me, if no one minds."

"No, of course not, it's your call," replied Claire, obviously relieved that I had accepted this decision relatively calmly. "If you could just let Jenny know who will be coming so that she can finalise the list of attendees for the undertakers.."

"Yes, I understand. I'll see you next Saturday then."

"I'll email you to confirm all the times and let you have the Zoom link. Bye for now."

I went to find Andrew, who was overseeing some gardening work in the churchyard.

"The daffodils do look lovely at this time of year. An outdoor service next week will be a real tonic if the weather plays ball," I greeted him.

"We've made good progress this morning tidying up the borders. How's your morning been?"

"Well, I've just been speaking to Claire. There's only space for two from our family at the funeral next week. We need to decide who should go with me ... you or James. I think James will want to go as he spent so much time with Richard when he was working in Stafford during his intern year. And the funeral's on Easter Saturday."

"Easter Saturday? How on earth are they going to make sure the building's safe for Sunday morning?" Andrew exclaimed. "Still, that's not my problem. If you're sure about travelling on your own, I really don't mind James going instead of me. I've been to more than my fair share of funerals over the last twelve months."

"I'll check out the trains. I was thinking about driving to Exeter and then getting the through train to Stafford." Andrew frowned. "I know it's riskier from a COVID point of view, but I really don't like the thought of driving all that way up the M5 on my own. The train could well be quicker and there may not be too many people travelling, it's not as if it's a normal Bank Holiday week-end."

"No, you're right. Although if you wanted, I could drive and just wait for you."

"I'll be fine on my own. You'll have plenty to do here I expect."

"Nothing Maisie couldn't manage," replied Andrew wryly. "But you decide."

"Thank you. Now, can I do anything to help with these borders?"

A stint of gardening did wonders for my mood. I checked out the train times and made arrangements to meet James at Stafford Station the following Saturday. I appreciated Andrew's offer to travel with me up to the Midlands but eventually decided that I would rather be on my own.

The following week passed in the same way as so many others this year: sessions at the vaccination centre, a few walks along the coastal path on fine days, online Pilates, family catch ups on Zoom and the inevitable myriad queries for Andrew in the run up to the reopening of the church for public worship. The number of COVID cases continued to fall and a gradual relaxation of restrictions was promised, albeit too late for the Easter Bank Holiday week end, during which North Devon would be unusually quiet for a second year.

Richard's funeral was a surreal experience, a small gathering in a large, draughty church building followed by the burial, sandwiched between two long train journeys. I arrived home to find Andrew shuffling through a pile of lists.

"How did it go? I'm glad to see you back in such good time. As far as I could tell on Zoom, everyone was sitting well apart and the Church Wardens seemed to handle marshalling people in and out very well. The children made a good job of the eulogy, not too over the top and a few jokes Richard would have enjoyed."

"Yes, they coped very well, Jenny should be proud of them. I don't think even you could have found fault with the undertakers, they were well aware of all the rules, but sympathetic at the same time."

"That's good to hear, you don't need anything to make a difficult day worse."

"No, and the trains were all punctual too. Anyway, what have you been up to? Is everything sorted for tomorrow?"

"Well, yes, but I was just checking the lists and I can't find your name on either of them."

I racked my brains. "I didn't book, oh, I'm sorry Andrew. With all the arrangements for the funeral, I just didn't think about having to book for an Easter Service here."

"Well, I suppose we could squeeze you in ... "

"No, no, I won't let you bend the rules for me. It really wouldn't be right for the Church Warden's wife to get special treatment. Maybe if I come to the outdoor service and stand away from the lawn, I could still hear what's going on."

"Are you sure?" said Andrew, looking relieved. "If someone cries off, I can give you a space."

"That's sorted then."

The sun was already shining brightly the following morning as I made my way to church. I had left as late as possible to avoid having to explain to people why I was standing on my own and I could hear a recording of "Jesus Christ is risen today" being played as I entered the churchyard. A circle of small groups of people stood on the lawn in front of the church, maintaining their "social bubbles". What a year it had been, and the prospect of "normal life" still seemed remote.

On the bank behind me, a remnant of an old hedgerow, the primroses were opening in the warm spring sunshine, just as they always did. I started to think ahead; if the government's plans to ease restrictions stayed on schedule, a family party to celebrate Andrew's 70th birthday in July might just be possible.

# APPENDIX

*A brief chronology of the COVID lockdowns and restrictions in the UK from February 2020 to March 2021*

**February 2020**

Reports of a lockdown in the Chinese city of Wuhan started to dominate the news. The Chinese authorities had imposed severe restrictions on movement in an effort to curtail the spread of a new virus known as COVID 19. However, due to the global nature of trade and tourism, the virus had already spread westward and there was a significant outbreak of cases in northern Italy which threatened to overwhelm health services there.

**March 2020**

The number of COVID cases in the UK started to increase. At this stage, those infected were required to isolate themselves and public health authorities endeavoured to trace other individuals with whom they had come into close contact.

The government's initial approach was to try to slow down the spread of the virus, even as lockdowns were introduced in other western European countries. The public were advised that whilst for most people, the effects of the virus would be mild, for the elderly and those with underlying health conditions, it was far more serious and could result in severe breathing difficulties. The death rate was estimated at 2%. The virus was readily transmissible either through close contact, defined as being less than two metres from a person for more than ten minutes, or through touching infected surfaces. The public were advised to take additional hygiene measures, including frequent and thorough handwashing and disposal of face tissues; the advice was summarised in the phrase "Catch it, bin it, kill it."

By mid-March, this position was no longer sustainable and on

16 March, the public were advised to avoid all unnecessary social contacts and travel. It was becoming increasingly difficult to keep schools open.

On 23 March, the Prime Minister, Boris Johnson, announced stringent lockdown measures to take immediate effect. The public were required to stay at home except for going out to do essential shopping and for daily exercise. All other shops, places of worship, leisure facilities and hospitality venues had to close. The over 70s were advised to "self-isolate" whilst those identified as being "extremely clinically vulnerable" were required to "shield", that is, to remain at home. Schools were only open for children of "key workers" such as NHS staff and teachers; employees were advised to work from home if possible. Within shops that remained open, customers were advised to shop on their own and "social distancing" measures were introduced to reduce the risk of close contact.

The Chancellor announced support for businesses, with the main measure being "furlough" payments. The government paid 80% of wage costs for employees who were unable to work because of the COVID restrictions. There were grants for the self-employed.

The lockdown measures were broadly similar in England, Scotland, Wales and Northern Ireland although each administration remained responsible for the specific measures in their jurisdiction. The Scottish and Welsh governments tended to adopt a more cautious approach to easing restrictions than their English counterparts.

The government instituted daily press conferences with three speakers (typically a government minister, a public health official and an NHS official) to provide updates on COVID case numbers, deaths, hospital admissions and "road maps" out of lockdown.

## April 2020

The number of COVID deaths increased to a peak of between 600 and 700 per day. The number of deaths in care homes was a particular source of concern, as patients with COVID were discharged from hospitals into care homes. COVID testing was still very limited.

There were shortages of some basic foods as a result of panic buying, and of items such as flour because of the popularity of home baking.

There was a boom in online video conferencing, with many educational resources available online. The personal fitness trainer Joe Wicks broadcast daily work outs for children which were extremely popular.

Social activities also moved online using "Zoom", an online video conferencing tool; from choir rehearsals to fitness classes, church services to family quizzes, technology had a major impact in reducing the isolation of lockdowns.

**May 2020**

Some easing of restrictions was announced as employers were encouraged to re-open workplaces if their employees could not work from home. Workers were encouraged to avoid using public transport. In addition, lower risk activities which took place predominantly outdoors or where social distancing measures were practicable were permitted; this included the re- opening of garden centres which would otherwise have lost a season's stock and golf courses (but not the associated hospitality facilities).

In England, travel for outdoor recreation was no longer restricted to the immediate local area and crowds converged on beaches in good weather. However, English residents were not permitted to travel to Wales or Scotland for outdoor leisure activities.

**June 2020**

Primary schools re opened, although the extent of the re-opening varied. Social distancing measures had to be put in place and outdoor activities were strongly encouraged.

Non-essential shops re opened on June 15.

Places of worship re opened on June 15 for private prayer and funerals. There was a limit of 30 on the number allowed to attend a funeral.

The government introduced social "support bubbles", allowing adults who lived alone to mix without restriction with another household; for example, a single grandparent could visit the home of an adult child and their family. If anyone in the social bubble tested positive for COVID, all members of the bubble had to self-isolate.

## July 2020

Places of worship in England were allowed to open for public worship from 4 July, with appropriate social distancing measures. Congregational singing was not permitted.

Indoor hospitality venues and hairdressers were allowed to re-open with reduced social distancing provided that other measures were in place: these included wearing face coverings when not seated.

All of these indoor venues had to maintain records of customers so that close contacts of anyone who subsequently tested positive for COVID could be advised to self-isolate; this was known as "track and trace recording". The NHS developed a track and trace app which could be used as an alternative with visitors checking in to a venue using its unique QR Code.

After much debate, it became mandatory to wear face coverings on public transport, in health and social care settings, shops, cinemas and places of worship from 24 July.

The number of COVID cases continued to fall and the requirement for those who were extremely clinically vulnerable to "shield" ended.

## August 2020

The Chancellor Rishi Sunak announced the "Eat out to help out" scheme to encourage the public to visit indoor hospitality venues. Under the scheme, the price of food and non-alcoholic beverages attracted a 50% government subsidy of up to £10 per person for sales from Monday to Thursday.

**September 2020**

As society opened up, including a full return to schools and universities, the number of COVID cases and hospital admissions began to rise relentlessly.

In England, a limit of six was placed on the size of a group that could meet together socially, and more stringent restrictions were introduced in areas of the country where case rates were higher.

On 22 September, the government advised that employees should return to home working if possible and introduced a 10pm curfew for hospitality venues.

**October 2020**

On 14 October, a three tier system of restrictions was put in place in England, with differing levels of restriction on hospitality venues and travel depending on the level of cases in a local authority. This was soon followed on 30 October by the announcement of a second lockdown, to take effect from 2 November. The major difference from the first lockdown was that schools remained open, although the high level of COVID cases resulted in significant levels of absence given the requirement for social bubbles to self-isolate after a positive test result. Within schools, classes, and in some cases, whole year groups, formed social bubbles.

More workplaces remained open as employers had implemented social distancing measures and revised working practices earlier in the year.

**November 2020**

Despite the lockdown, case numbers in England reached higher levels than previously recorded, although the level of testing also continued to increase. A new and more transmissible variant of the COVID virus known as the "Alpha" variant was identified in south east England, but like subsequent variants, it quickly spread throughout the country.

On November, the first COVID vaccine developed by Pfizer BioNTech was approved by the UK regulatory authorities, followed by a second vaccine, developed by Astra Zeneca. The race was on to vaccinate the population as quickly as possible, starting with care home residents and staff, NHS staff and the oldest age groups in the wider population.

The leaders of the four home nations met to agree on what degree of mixing would be allowed over the Christmas period; it was decided that up to three households would be allowed to meet together at once over the period from 23 to 27 December.

## December 2020

As lockdown was lifted, concerns remained about the high level of COVID cases. The tier system remained in place in England.

In the South East, a return to higher levels of restrictions tantamount to lockdown was announced on December 19, which meant that residents could not travel to spend Christmas with relatives in other parts of the country and vice versa. The five- day relaxation of the rules on social mixing that had been announced in November was replaced with a relaxation for a single day only.

In Wales and Scotland there was a return to full lockdown immediately after Christmas; England followed on 6 January.

## January to March 2021

The whole country remained in lockdown as the race to vaccinate the population gathered pace. Vaccination centres were created at venues large and small, from village halls to sports stadia, involving recruitment of large numbers of volunteers to assist with administration and marshalling. The number of people hospitalised due to COVID peaked in January and the death rate peaked at an average of over 1,000 per day that month.

In contrast to the first lockdown, places of worship were not required to close, although many did and decisions on the timing and extent of re-opening were made locally. Many churches were re- opened for public worship, albeit with social distancing measures still in place and without congregational singing, for Easter Sunday, which fell on April 4.

The government's priority when restrictions eased was to re- open schools; in England, schools opened again on 8 March and other restrictions were gradually eased from late March 2021. By July, all restrictions apart from the wearing of face coverings, had been lifted.

Printed in Great Britain
by Amazon